SWORN

MARIA LUIS

SWORN

BLOOD DUET, BOOK 1

MARIA LUIS

ALKMINI BOOKS, LLC

I bow to no man.

The words are tattooed on my skin, just as they're branded on my heart.

But I never planned for Sergeant Lincoln Asher, a man as deceptive as he is cold. His dominance sets my teeth on edge . . . and my body on fire. He won't stop until I'm his, but I'm not his to take.

My secrets bind me—and blind me.

I live in the shadows of New Orleans. Hidden and protected in the underworld I call home. I know who I am.

I vow never to kneel before a man...

Save one.

And he will be my downfall.

Cover Photographer: James Critchley

Cover Model: Charlie Garforth

Cover Designer: Najla Qamber, Najla Qamber Designs

Editing: Kathy Bosman, Indie Editing Chick

Proofreading: Tandy Proofreads

❀ Created with Vellum

To Panic! At The Disco:
Thank you for the amazing-ness that is Don't Threaten Me With A Good Time. I'm pretty sure the Blood Duet wouldn't have been written without this song - to date, I've listened to it 867 times, which means...2,887 minutes later, it only seemed right that this book be dedicated to you, since you've (technically) been along for the journey anyway. No song could have been a better fit for Lincoln & Avery.

⚜

⚜

Good job, honey.

PROLOGUE

AVERY

The death was not mine to see.

    The tremble in my knees told me that.

The slick sweat on my palms told me that.

The—

Heavy boots moved along the corridor, echoing against the hardwood flooring, and I sank to the ground, behind a wall, away and out of sight. My arms locked around my shins, my crooked nose buried between my bent knees.

Don't breathe. Don't breathe. Don't—

"Where is she?"

That voice.

It was sickening the way that I found a measure of calm in hearing him speak. Sickening because he'd given the order to have Momma murdered—calm because his voice had been the center of my world since I'd entered preschool. Helping me into my school uniform, reminding me to brush my teeth at night, pouring me a bowl of cereal in the morning when Momma slept in too late, the vodka bottle cradled to her chest like a newborn babe.

He killed her, and he'll kill you too.

He would. I knew he would.

I lifted my face from the safety of my jean-clad knees and surveyed my familiar surroundings.

"How the *fuck* do you not know where she is?"

"She cracked open the window in her bedroom," said an unfamiliar male voice. "What the fuck did you want me to do? Follow her out and drag her back in here? Or finish off the job you wanted from me and kill your wife?"

Breathe, breathebreathebreathe.

I'd come back for Momma after the man had locked my door. I'd heard her screams. I'd heard her pain. I'd been halfway across the front lawn, already circling to the other side of the house to another entrance, when I'd heard the gunshot that drove me to my knees and pulled the vomit from my body.

"Find her."

"Is she worth all this? You've done her mother in. You that much of a sick bastard that you want your thirteen-year-old stepdaughter dead for shit that—"

The sound of flesh hitting the wall sounded like the pistol used against Momma.

Loud.

Startling.

Furious.

"If I *wanted* your fucking opinion, I'd ask for it. You hear me?"

There was no fight, no struggle.

Only the harsh sound of my breath quickening against my interlaced fingers, and then the soft, dangerous laugh of a man who welcomed death. "You gonna kill me, too, Jay? You going to use the same gun on me that I used on your wife? You gonna fuck me up because I let your precious stepdaughter slip away?"

Nothing.

Nothing.

Nothing.

And then the blinding crack of a pistol erupted like thunder across a hot New Orleans summer day.

I felt that inferno.

I felt the heat and the rage and the fear of the unnamed man who hadn't chased me, even though I'd spotted his silhouette in my bedroom window.

This time, I didn't throw up.

I scrambled to my feet, using the opportunity of the man's death and my stepfather's distraction to make my escape from the only home I'd ever known. I ran. And I ran.

And I didn't stop until the soles of my bare feet were scraped raw from the cement, and there were no thoughts left of Momma, or my stepfather, or the man who'd let me live.

There was nothingness—a black void that swept over me and sucked me down into the abyss.

It wasn't until the sun peaked out over the horizon the following morning that I realized I'd found harbor just outside the iron gates of Lafayette Cemetery #1 on Washington Avenue.

I'd entered my own slice of purgatory, just like Mrs. Holland had taught us about in religion class last week. But this time, I had no indulgences of my own to buy my way into heaven.

I had nothing.

I had no one.

And I suspected that if I wanted to live another day, I had to *become* no one.

1

AVERY

In the bowel of New Orleans, I was the gatekeeper to the no-longer living.

The woman seated across from me leaned in, elbow resting on my rickety fold-up table. One manicured finger tapped the Death card, little puffs of smoke curling from her mouth as she sucked on a Marlboro Red like it was something a whole lot dirtier.

"I'm gonna die, aren't I?" Her cheeks hollowed out around the cigarette as she spoke. "This right here? Skeleton can't be any good, Miss Washington, can't be any damn good."

Tarot was an art I'd picked up from the other readers in Jackson Square years earlier. For me, it was a means to an end. I lacked the Sight that my peers possessed in spades. I lacked their ability to look at a card and see a tangled web of lust, lies, and love—I saw the cards' illustrations, knew their meanings from years of study, and wasn't opposed to taking a little creative liberty.

The better the reading, the higher the tip, which nicely

padded the conservative fee I charged to encourage people to come to my table as opposed to one of the others.

In other words, survival of the fittest.

"No, ma'am," I purred in a throaty voice, "not death."

Her shoulders sagged with relief.

"Not always, anyway." Her eyes went wide and, hiding a victorious grin, I shuffled the Thoth deck and selected another card from its midst. "The Death card symbolizes regrowth, a new change. The shedding of the old and the gradual shift into the new." Turning the fresh card onto its back, settling it next to Death, I offered a genuine smile. "Lust, ma'am. Are you newly single?"

The woman's mouth dropped open, her cigarette dangling. Even within the shadows of the towering St. Louis Cathedral, there was no mistaking her pink cheeks and rapid blinking. "Divorced." She plucked the Red from her mouth and stomped it out on the cobblestones beside my table. "How'd you know that?"

Because I've seen you before.

Not *her*, obviously, but women like her. Men, too. They all carried that faraway gaze—some more cynical than others—that spoke to the man-made hell called marriage. A trap society whispered that you needed, that you should crave above all else.

I didn't crave marriage.

Hell, I barely craved men at all—living on the streets for most of my teenage years meant that my breasts had been pawed at by disgusting assholes, my ass grabbed, and I'd been told one too many times that I was such a pretty girl and wouldn't I look so damn good on my knees?

I'd be dead before I ever got on my knees for a man.

I hummed a sound of faux excitement in my throat, stroking a finger along the crisp edge of Lust. "The cards, ma'am. You've clearly come to N'Orleans for something new. You wish to get lost, and yes"—I pointed to the first card I'd selected, the Queen of Disks—"you're prepared to spend some money on what you want. Disks represent external items. Material possessions, money, that sort of thing. But I would caution you against leaning too heavily into lust."

Her eyes tracked the motion of my hands as I packed the cards against one palm and set them all down. "I want to be wanted." Her hushed tone hardly concealed her wistfulness. "I want to *feel* again."

"Don't we all?"

At that, she blinked and pulled back, arms locking around her belly. Her chin tipped to the right, her gaze flicking to the line of Tarot readers bordering the square. It was a Saturday night, which meant money. Lots of it, if we did our job correctly—and clearly, I'd failed to live up to expectation.

She wanted the lies, the promise that she'd meet her "one and only" during her time in New Orleans. She just plain old *wanted*, and either I played the game and walked away with cash in my pocket or I went back to my apartment and stressed over making rent this month.

Put aside the guilt and tell her what she wants to hear.

Do it, Avery, just do it.

Self-hatred settled like soured milk in my stomach, as did the heavy reminder that I was no one. I had no family and few friends. I left little trace of my existence, save for the sight of my face as I strolled through the French Quarter. Runners like me were a dime a dozen in New Orleans, but even knowing that didn't erase my bitterness for what could have been.

Avery Washington was just one alias I'd chosen in the last twelve years. I'd been Samantha Lovelace for most of my teens—a naïve little idiot who placed her trust in all the wrong people. Ruby Matheson during the year that I'd turned twenty—a little more jaded, but no less of an idiot.

It took me awhile to realize that people sought to protect their own interests, and no one gave a damn about mine.

I'd become Avery Washington ever since I'd caught sight of a suspicious-looking man following me home one night, sing-songing my name like he wouldn't mind taking me into a dark alley and abusing my body for his pleasure. He'd been a stranger who stalked the readers in the square before being arrested on an assault charge. Even after the cuffs were locked around his wrists, I'd been terrified to walk the shadowed streets alone. But there'd been no one to protect me then just as there was no one to protect me now.

A name change did only so much.

Ice skittered up my spine, and the self-hatred slipped away.

I met the woman's eyes, ignoring the flash of hope in their depths. "You'll meet him." Her soft gasp bounced off my steel heart. "You'll meet him exactly as you envision, and you'll be *wanted*, ma'am, just as you dream." With hardened resolve, I tapped the Queen of Disks card once more. "But love will continue to elude you if you focus on the material things. Seek more than just the external, and you'll discover the man who waits for you."

"But where will I *find* him?"

It was with a sense of good timing that the bells of St. Louis Cathedral chimed on the hour. Midnight.

"Church. You'll meet him at church."

The woman's lips peeled back in a grimace, revealing crowded front teeth. "I don't *go* to church."

"If you want to meet this man, you will."

She didn't like that, I could tell. But aside from casting a quick glance at the imposing structure behind her, she didn't fight back. Her fingers dipped into her purse, scrounging around for what I hoped was my tip.

A crinkled dollar bill fluttered to the table.

Clearly, I shouldn't have taken inspiration from my surroundings.

"Have a good night."

She didn't return the sentiment, only drew up her jacket and hunched her shoulders as she skirted around the other readers. I watched as she gave a little jump when a homeless man sat up on a wrought-iron bench and stuck out a tin can in her direction.

I didn't need to hear her to know that she'd responded with something offensive.

The man reared back, can to his chest, his expression lost to the moonless night sky, and I felt the familiar stirring of anger.

I had been that man, begging for a dime, a sandwich, a scrap of hope.

My knees cracked as I stood, my flimsy lawn chair teetering on its hind legs before I settled a hand on the dirty fabric and righted it again.

Don't. Don't go over there and get in someone else's business.

The woman's voice carried on the upwind breeze: "Don't *touch* me, asshole."

Yeah, there was no way I could let that slide. It was one thing to ignore the man, to step around him and lift your chin and pretend he didn't exist.

Another thing entirely to make eye contact and act like a dick.

"Avery."

Involuntarily, my shoulders twitched at the sound of my name coming off the lips of my regular neighbor, Tabitha.

Didn't matter that I'd been "Avery" for three years now, sometimes I still didn't answer when called. *You aren't Laurel anymore, just remember that.*

Easier said than done.

"You might want to go home."

"Why?" I met Tabby's gaze. "You hear something?"

She touched her chest, right over her permit, and then pointed in the same direction my client had taken.

The woman had moved on from the homeless man and had stopped to talk to a different guy. The flickering gas lamps did nothing to hide his imposing physique—tall, broad, narrow waist. He stood like a soldier or a cop or *anyone*, really, that I did not want on my radar.

With one hand latched onto his arm, the woman turned back and . . . pointed. At *me*.

Oh, shit.

"Get out of here, Ave."

Yeah, Tabby didn't have to tell me twice.

That was sort of the thing about operating a Tarot card stand illegally on Jackson Square. I wouldn't recommend the no-permit stint, but hey, I'd managed to do well enough for the last few years.

The pin of my fake badge stuck me in the breast as I jerked my chair closed and shoved the table's accessories into my backpack. Candle (unlit), Tarot cards, crystals, pendulum. The backpack's zipper sounded unnaturally loud when it jammed, and I tugged, and—*screw it.*

I slung the strap over one shoulder.

Grabbed the chair by one pointy leg.

Made a hasty swipe of the plush-velvet tablecloth and tossed the heavy fabric over my arm.

Time to go.

Implausible as it was, the air seemed to thicken as he

stepped up behind me like some sort of crazy scene out of a horror movie.

A masculine hand landed on my shoulder, fingers broad and strong.

I didn't scream—I'm *not* a screamer.

But all words stuck in my throat, and then there was nothing but the sound of his baritone drawl.

"Going somewhere?"

She looked like she'd seen a ghost.

Then again, she'd spotted me—and I was as close to dead as a man with a pulse could be.

"Going somewhere?"

Her shoulder tensed under my hand, and I pulled back. I was a heartless bastard, but even I didn't get my rocks off on frightening the vulnerable. And this girl . . . I lowered my gaze to her trim form. She was thin, almost too thin, though her loose-fitting skirt and the equally billowy shirt didn't do her any favors.

If she had even the slightest hint of curves under all that fabric, I couldn't tell worth a damn.

"In a hurry?"

Fingers turning white as she clutched the strap of her backpack, she faced me. Full-on. Eyes on my face, unwavering, chin tipped up at an angle.

Fuck. Me.

Her body might be lost to the tent of her clothes, but her face was another story. Gorgeous, despite the drawn lines of her dark brows and her pursed, angry mouth. That mouth of hers was fantasy material—full and pink and lush, the sort men spent their nights jerking off to in the hope that, one day, they'd wake up and have it wrapped around their cock.

From the way her hazel eyes flashed, I'd venture a guess and say *that* particular fantasy was nothing but a pipe dream.

"I have an appointment."

Her throaty voice jerked my eyes back down to her mouth. Jesus, but the sound was like velvet. Tempting. Sexy. Haunting. The perfect melody to hear after a night of back-clawing, hard sex.

Shaking myself from the vivid reverie, I focused on the anger. Her anger. I'd long ago learned to live with my own. "You have an appointment at midnight?" I'd been a cop long enough to recognize even the best bull-shitters. "Really."

Hazel eyes narrowed on me, her mouth flat-lining another degree. "You going to arrest me?"

Something about the way she'd ID'ed me, even with a nondescript jacket drawn over my Class B's, made me feel as though she'd had her fair of run-ins with the NOPD in the past. To say nothing of the fact that her jaded attitude mirrored my own.

Slipping my hands into the front pockets of my navy-blue, department-issued slacks, I cocked my head toward the other vendors. "There've been a few calls about harassment lately. Juveniles, mostly." I paused, waiting for her to cut me some slack. One second passed, and then the moment bled into another. On my third breath, I demolished the silence, like a roach beneath my shoe, and spoke: "Wanted to do a quick walk-through of the square before heading home for the night. Make sure no one was having any trouble."

Not even a hint of a relieved smile softened her expression.

I didn't blame her for the suspicion. Hell, there wasn't a single soul on this planet that I trusted not to stab me in the back the moment I looked away. It came with the territory of living double lives—of playing two sides of the same coin, always fully aware that one wrong move could end with my throat slit and my body tossed into the swamp.

It was the reality of my life.

At thirty-four, I knew nothing else.

When the woman turned, dismissing me, I withdrew my wallet from my back pocket. Flipped it open and removed my police identification card like that would help me earn some street cred with her. "Sergeant Lincoln Asher." I held out the ID, the back of my hand accidentally grazing her breast.

Or where her breast *ought* to be, but again, her tent-like shirt concealed everything.

It *didn't* conceal the way her jaw worked tightly, though. Nor the hard swallow that slid down the length of her neck before she snapped, "I don't care who you are."

No, she clearly didn't.

The feeling wasn't mutual. And that was . . . unusual, really fucking unusual.

The ID went back into my wallet, and the wallet back into my pocket. "You been reading cards for a while?"

"If you're going to arrest me, Sergeant, just do it."

"I'm not going to arrest you." Although maybe there was a reason why I should. *No one* put up a fuss like this woman had in the span of five minutes unless she'd done something bad and more than a little illegal. "So," I said, drawing out the *O*, "you read."

As if resigned to her fate, she dropped her backpack

onto the crooked table and then let the chair clatter to her feet. A piece of paper fell from the unzipped backpack. Dark as the evening was, there was no mistaking the scribbles across the page.

"Are you trying to ask me if I'm a fraud?" she demanded.

I couldn't tear my gaze from the leaflet. Instinct had me itching to reach for it, to hold it up to the scant light from the reproduction gas lamps and see what the hell she'd written down so furiously that her words didn't even stay on the correct lines. "I don't know. Are you?"

"No."

"All right then."

She shifted, her elbow knocking into the backpack. More papers floated out, along with two worn-down candles.

"Shit," she cursed, the word leaving on a breathy sigh.

Curiosity may have killed the cat, but I figured I had at least another two lives left in me—and no way would this slip of a woman have the chance to steal one.

"Let me get that for you." *Yeah, just play the gentleman card like you give a shit.* I didn't, and maybe tomorrow I'd wake up and wonder why I'd pushed this woman's buttons. Maybe tomorrow I'd remind myself that I wasn't in a position to wonder about this woman's jaded air or her pink, fuckable lips, or the way she looked at me as though she *knew* that I was no good.

That my heart was as cold and impenetrable as the cobblestones we stood on.

Right now, though, I didn't think.

I bent, my knees popping from years of excruciating labor, and I snagged the papers straight from her grip. Like the asshole I was, I lifted them well above her head so that I could read the words scrawled in perfectly imperfect chicken-scratch.

What in the—

I flipped to the next page.

To the next.

And to the next.

"You a stalker, ma'am?" I kept my voice cool, easy.

"I'm not . . ." A growl escaped her lips, and she made a hasty swipe at my hand. Fuck that. My hold on the leaflets went iron-tight as she blew out a frustrated breath. "I'm not a stalker."

"Then why"—I curled the stack in one fist, dipping my chin to meet her eyes—"do you have notes on at least five of my officers?"

The blood drained from her face, and this time when she swallowed, I knew she tasted fear. "I don't . . ." Her tongue swiped out in a nervous gesture, touching the cushion of her bottom lip. "It's not just police officers."

"No?"

"No, I-I—" Eyes slamming shut, she counted to ten, if the way her mouth silently formed the numbers was any indication. Then she looked at me again, and I felt lust spear me, unwanted and misplaced because while I'd done some fucked-up shit in my life, I still had boundaries. Screwing a woman who noticed the minute details was not in my future. Ever.

Visibly swallowing, she finally ground out, "I watch people, okay? It's a-a *thing* for me."

"Like a voyeur."

"What? *No.*" She pointed at the papers, and then reached into her backpack for her tarot cards. Holding them up with a little wiggle, she muttered, "I take notes, all right?

On the people who visit my table and have me read their cards. *Only* ever on them."

Adrenaline grasped my lungs, heaving a deep breath from my chest. I needed to stop the trajectory of my thoughts. Hell, I needed to walk away and go the fuck home. It'd been a long night. Long and unforgiving, and not because of the shift I'd pulled for the NOPD.

For everything else.

Everything else I wasn't allowed to say, and everything else I would never repeat to another human soul.

The deck clasped tight in her hands drew my attention. "You never tell anyone what you hear?"

Uncomfortable silence stretched between us before her throaty voice answered, "It's for me. I . . . I analyze patterns in what's told to me."

She was a shit liar, but she could keep those secrets of hers to herself.

"Read me."

"Excuse me?"

"My cards." I lifted my gaze to her face. Shock resided in those hazel eyes of hers, as did blatant distrust. She was right not to trust me—that was a fact. I cleared my throat. "Read my cards."

"Absolutely not."

Lifting a brow, I murmured, "Scared?"

"Of *you*?" Disbelief coated her tone like thick honey.

"You see anyone else standing here?" At her silence, I folded my arms over my chest. "Read my cards . . . unless maybe you *are* nervous, just a little bit."

Her teeth worked her bottom lip, and I wouldn't be surprised if she broke the skin. "You don't scare me."

"Don't I?" I tested her words, taking a step toward her and

breeching her space. But she surprised me—for all the lip-nibbling and the stammering, she didn't budge and she sure as hell didn't retreat. Defiance radiated from every inch of her.

It was more of a turn-on than I'd like to admit. Worse, it made me curious. Who had broken her spirit so badly that her armor was as thick as my own? I didn't have the answer, but the longer she stood there, with her hands balled into fists and her eyes narrowed into slits, the more I wanted to dredge the truth from her lips.

No matter that it wasn't any of my business.

"No one scares me," she said.

Another lie, but I wouldn't press her on it.

I only studied her, allowing my silence to bait her into giving in. *Patience, man, have patience.*

Three . . .

Two . . .

One—

"*Fine.*" With a hard glare, she slipped the cards from their velvet pouch and shuffled them with sharp motions. "Two cards. Your past and your future."

"What about my present?"

The shuffling slowed, then stalled completely. "It doesn't matter. In a moment, this will be your past too."

I wanted to tell her that she looked too damn young to be spouting out that sort of wisdom. But was she really that young? It was too dark to tell, her features lost to the shadows, and she didn't give me the opportunity to give it another thought.

She cut the deck, wrists moving fluidly. Selected a card from the middle and held it up, allowing the sparse moonlight to reveal the image. I wrangled in the urge to snag it from her grasp and hurry up the process.

"Ruin."

My chin jerked back. "Excuse me?"

"Ruin," she reiterated, voice soft but unyielding, "it's the Ten of Swords."

"I have no idea what that means."

Her teeth audibly clacked together. "I'm aware, Sergeant. Ruin—it's a card in the Minor Arcana." She flicked her nail against the card, and then turned it toward me. In the slight shadows, all that remained visible was the color red and what looked to be a sword with a myriad of other, smaller swords piercing the largest one. "It represents a period of endless fighting, a struggle that you can't win."

This was a bad idea.

Maybe she was a fraud—in that moment, I hoped it was true. I hoped that she'd lied to every single person who had ever sat at her table here in Jackson Square because I refused to believe that everything I had worked toward in the last thirty-four years had been for nothing.

My fingers sank into my dark hair, my palm following the curve of my skull to where I'd been branded like cattle years ago.

Hazel eyes met mine. "With no hope, your past has led to your destruction."

I opened my mouth to speak. Or maybe I only thought that I did.

There were no words—only blood. The blood I had spilled and the blood that I had given. Not for the first time in my life, I felt dirty, rotten, all the way to my soul. And *hopeless*, like there was no end to the struggle and to the pain and to the goddamn detachment I forced upon myself so that I could do what I needed to do and not consider the consequences of my actions.

"Interested in your future?" she asked apathetically, already swiping another card from the deck.

No, I wanted to yell. If Ruin was my past, then there was no telling what the hell my—

"Death." She turned the card around to show me. "Your future is Death."

And as I stood there woodenly, my fucking brain trying to wrap around the reality of my existence, she gathered her belongings and swept off into the night.

Leaving me alone.

As I'd always been.

3

AVERY

I'd lied to Sergeant Lincoln Asher.

Oh, not about the cards I'd picked for him. Not exactly, anyway.

But I'd allowed him to believe that he was doomed, past and future, that there was no hope left for him to believe in. If anything, the Death card marked a turning point in his future, where something inherently good, no doubt, waited just around the bend.

Except he'd made me feel uncomfortable. He was too rugged, too forward, too in-your-face masculine, and in a split-second decision, I'd sought to force his weight off the proverbial seesaw and set my queen directly in front of his king. *Checkmate.*

Curiosity led me to pull yet another card for him on my way back to my apartment.

His present.

Cruelty.

Whenever I felt the sharp blades of long-standing hate seep into my bones, I pulled out my deck and chose a card. And *always* the card was Cruelty—in other words, the constant analyzing and deciphering which inevitably ended in nothingness.

Tabitha once explained the card to a client as a person lost in a maze. No matter how many times you peered over the uncut hedges, no matter how many times you retraced your steps, all of your work always led you to . . . nothing.

Cruelty was a mind-game, so it made sense that I'd been pulling the same card now for four years. Before that, even, if you counted the number of times one of the readers in the square rolled out a spread for me—long before I'd ever picked up a deck myself.

But why would Sergeant Asher play mind-games?

With a glance over my shoulder at the empty street, my fingers stole under my too-big shirt for the key I'd hooked onto a chain around my neck. The French Quarter may have been my home for the last twelve years, but I wasn't ignorant to its many ghosts, those of fictitious rumors and others which were firmly rooted in reality.

Too much went unseen in New Orleans for me to ever feel truly safe.

Keying the antique door open, I slipped inside the multi-apartment, nineteenth-century building and locked everything up behind me. I lived in what New Orleans' legend called the Sultan's Palace, a home of alleged brutality and death and chopped-up human parts.

No part of the tall tale was true, and the only reason I'd agreed to live here, at the corner of Dauphine and Orleans, was because the rent was cheap and the landlord didn't ask questions.

Lugging my belongings up to the third floor without an elevator was annoying but habit at this point. My fold-up chairs bounced against the outside of my leg, and my backpack hung low on my shoulder. The table had been left behind—hopefully it'd be there tomorrow morning.

Would Sergeant Asher come back then?

I hoped not.

He'd been . . . I didn't know, really. Harsh, maybe? His face certainly had been. Even though I had pretty much no sex drive, I could recognize a good-looking guy when I saw one.

Lincoln Asher wasn't good-looking, not in the classical sense. Thick dark hair, as black as the Mississippi River at night, had been swept to the side. His nose, like mine, had clearly been broken at some point. Full lips that didn't tug up into a smile, not even once. A series of jagged scars that cut across the profile of the right side of his face.

The prettiest thing about him had been the color of his eyes—an icy blue that was an exact match to the underside of every porch ceiling in the city. Haint blue, it was called. A color that homeowners bought by the gallon to paint their porches with, so birds wouldn't nest, thinking it was the sky. Legend had it, however, that the custom was rooted in Voodoo—where porch ceilings were painted blue, the color of water, so that spirits couldn't trespass into the home.

In Sergeant Asher's eyes, I'd seen nothing but the ghosts of his past.

The man was dangerous, self-destruction in wait, and I couldn't lie and say that I wasn't exactly the same.

Didn't mean we needed to step off the edge together, though.

"That you, Avery?"

I closed the apartment door with my elbow, still juggling everything in my arms. "Yeah, Katie, it's me."

Our apartment was miniscule, a whopping five-hundred-square-feet. You'd think we lived in Manhattan and not in New Orleans, but after three years, it was home. We had a single bedroom that belonged to Katie, a galley-style kitchen, a narrow bathroom, and a living room that seconded as a bedroom for me.

The apartment was in Katie's name, and she paid an extra hundred bucks on the rent each month. I would have given her the bedroom anyway—she often invited certain guests over, and the thought of walking in on naked asses and naked cocks and naked everything else didn't appeal to me.

Leave me to my pull-out couch and I was perfectly fine.

"How was the square?" she asked, coming into the living room from her bedroom. Dressed in shorts and an extra-large T-shirt, Katie's blond hair was a tangled mess on the top of her head. At my raised brows, she wiggled her own and hooked a thumb over one shoulder. *Company*, she mouthed, which said it all.

Guess I'd be making use of my headphones again tonight.

"It was fine. Had my fair share of people." I set all my stuff down behind the couch, so that they wouldn't be an eyesore for our *guest*. "A few regulars. Nothing too crazy."

Liar.

All right, so maybe I was itching to sit on the couch and record my night. I hadn't lied about that to the sergeant—I really did pay close attention to everyone who sat at my table. For the first few years after my mother's death, I'd done nothing but hide from my own shadow. A teenage girl in New Orleans, alone, was never a good idea. Slowly, as the initial fear had dissipated, everything came back to Jay Foley, my stepfather.

Now the current mayor of New Orleans.

So, I watched and I waited. Like tonight, no one could

resist having their cards read for long. I'd told the fortunes of lawyers and firefighters, of school teachers and strippers. I harbored the information away from all the pertinent people, always pushing the telling questions and patiently teasing out the answers from the darkest parts of their souls.

They all had secrets to hide, and I was particularly adept at uncovering their fears.

"Nobody bothered you, right?" Katie asked, leaning one shoulder against the door to her bedroom. "You know I worry."

Katie and I had met at the strip club a few years back. I'd gone with a client who promised me a good time after I'd finished his tarot reading, and I'd been desperate enough for human interaction that I'd agreed to go with him. Three hours later, my "date" had decided to wine and dine a tourist from Montana, and I'd drank one too many cocktails at the bar. Katie had lent me extra clothes when I'd puked all over myself, and she'd listened when I confessed that there had to be something wrong with me: no matter how many times I tried to let a man touch me, I couldn't.

"You a lesbian?" she'd asked after sipping on the salted rim of a margarita. "That's cool."

"I'm not a lesbian. I'm just like . . ." No words fit. How did I explain that what I wanted and needed were two different things? I needed men as a gender to stay far away from me, and, yet, I still *wanted* a man to get me off. Not that my brain ever turned off long enough for that to happen. "I'm me," I'd finally muttered pathetically.

Or rather, I was no one.

A figment of mashed identities, hoping to survive yet another day.

"I was good all night," I told Katie, refusing to meet her eye. If she caught onto the fact that I'd had a run-in with the

sergeant, she'd never let it go. "Is that"—I lowered my voice
—"George in there?"

Katie's mouth lifted in a wicked grin. "George *and* Tyler."

I laughed, not even scandalized by her overt sexuality.
Just because I was messed up in the head didn't mean my
roommate deserved to live the abstinent life right along with
me. "Get it, girl."

"I already have, and I plan to do so again. I keep trying to
convince them to, *you know*."

"Fight swords?"

Her blue eyes lit with humor. "Hell, I wish. At this point
I'm just hoping for a damn kiss between the two of them. It's
not every day you get two hot military dudes in your bed
at once."

I stepped behind my makeshift closet curtain and drew
it closed. Stripped off my work clothes—too-large items I'd
found at the thrift shop—and pulled on a pair of leggings
and a comfy sweater. "Something tells me that you're going
to have your way by the end of the night."

Katie's voice turned hopeful. "You pull a card for me?"

"The deck is in my backpack." I pushed the curtain to
the side. "But I can, if you want."

Biting her lip, she glanced back at her bedroom door. "I
think I might live the spontaneous life tonight."

"Live your best life," I teased, dropping onto the sofa.
"Promise them double penetration if they swap spit."

Katie's bark of laughter echoed in the living room. With
a shake of her head, she leaned forward over the back of the
couch and wrapped her arms around me for a hug. "Every
time I think you can't surprise me, you do, Avery. I just know
you're a kinky bitch under all those don't-touch-me vibes."

Kinky probably wasn't the best word for me—could
virgins be kinky?

According to books like *Fifty Shades of Grey*, yeah. According to my reality, I'd give it a hard hell-no.

I couldn't lower my guard long enough for a man to kiss me, never mind take out his dick and put it inside me. A romantic visual, I know, but I didn't have a romantic bone in my body.

Katie kissed the top of my head like I was a younger sister, which I guess I was. She was thirty-one to my twenty-five, and she was one of those suffocating affectionate people who believed hugs ought to be arm-delivered at least ten times a day.

In my ear, she whispered, "You'll meet the right guy for you, Aves. And I have a sneaking suspicion he'll be just as kinky as you."

Rolling my eyes, I shooed her away with my hands. She skipped back, a tinkling laugh emerging from her lips, before she swung the bedroom door open and announced, "All right, boys, who's up for a little D-P, huh?"

The door clicked shut behind her, and I drew in a deep breath. Katie didn't know my history, aside from the basics: I had no family; I'd dropped out of school at the age of thirteen; and I'd spent a large portion of my teenage years bouncing from one homeless shelter to another after Momma was murdered and I was left on my own.

Small as it was, this apartment in the Sultan's Palace was my most luxurious accommodation yet.

To the left of the couch was a small file cabinet, and I keyed open the top lock and removed a black binder, settling it on my thighs. Because of the whole no-school thing—teachers and administration asked too many questions—reading wasn't a pastime of mine. Still, a few years back I'd been riffling through the plastic baskets at the French Quarter Market, when I'd discovered a tiny picture

frame with a quote that might as well have struck
me dead:

*If you want to shine, New Orleans will let you thrive. But if
you want to hide who you really are, the city will keep your
secrets too.*

The words had kicked around in my head for days after,
taking root deep in my heart and spreading like wildfire.

New Orleans had hidden me; it had harbored me. And
now, it gave me the opportunity to discover the truth.

I slipped the binder open, traced the tiny, wooden
picture frame I'd squirreled away into my pocket all those
years ago, and then flipped past all of my notes.

Lawyers and firefighters, school teachers and strippers.

Whoever brought up Mayor Jay Foley, no matter if the
information was told to me in a positive or negative light,
went in the binder. His was a name on the tip of everyone's
tongues these days, now that he was up for reelection.

The man tonight had said nothing about my stepfather,
and yet for some reason I wanted to remember the cards I'd
picked for him. Ruin. Death.

Cruelty.

I wrote it all down, recalling those blue eyes of his and
the hard clench of his jaw. My pen scratched against the
paper, my crappy penmanship drifting across the page and
skipping out of the printed lines.

Sometimes, in life, you couldn't remain within the
confines.

I worried about that. I worried that I'd lived in the
shadows of New Orleans for too long and that I would never
have all of my answers unless I took that next step. My
palms grew sweaty at the thought. I had the courage to
watch Foley from afar, picking up information here and
there that could ruin him forever.

Whether I had the courage to do more than cling to the shadows—my safety net—remained to be seen.

My eyes fell shut, and I shoved aside the binder. Grabbing the throw blanket off the back of the coach, I wrapped it around my shoulders and stepped out onto our small balcony—another perk to living in the Quarter.

Three stories below, Dauphine Street was dimly lit. A group of tourists meandered down the way, arms wrapped around each other's shoulders, green Hand Grenade drinks clasped in tight fists.

"Gimme that! I need more."

"You always need more . . . in *bed*."

Their conversation floated up to the balcony, mingling with the jazz and rap music from Bourbon Street, one block over.

That could have been me.

Living life, hanging out with friends without having to constantly look over my shoulder. Maybe, twelve years after Momma's death, I should start thinking that Jay Foley had forgotten all about me, about his stepdaughter who'd escaped while he killed another man.

Under any other circumstances, I'd believe that it was all in my head and that I'd grown paranoid over the years.

But then I'd hear him on the radio or see him on TV. I'd listen as he fed the public lies and pretended that my mother had died of cancer, out of the public eye, and *not* with a single bullet straight to the back of her head, execution-style. I'd listen as he spun a tale of a touching scene with Momma surrounded by loved ones as she passed and not, as events had actually played out, alone in her dining room while her husband watched the blood soak the antique rug beneath her body. I'd listen as he pretended that *I* had been so distraught over my momma's death that

I'd spiraled into a depression and taken to inflicting self-harm.

"Laurel was a sweet, sweet girl, but there was nothing anyone could do to save her," he'd told the media. "I doubt she even realized what taking too many pills might do to her sweet, little body."

He'd effectively killed me without pulling the literal trigger.

And then he'd held a funeral, leveraging a body that was not mine into the Foley family tomb in St. Louis Cemetery #1 on Washington Avenue . . . exactly where I'd ended up, feet bleeding, a year earlier.

In that moment, at the age of fourteen, Laurel Peyton had ceased to exist.

A cry ripped through the night, high-pitched and keening, and the blanket fell from my shoulders to my feet.

Not Momma. It wasn't Momma.

Another cry, followed by deep, masculine grunting.

Right, Katie orgasming.

Not Momma dying.

Sometimes it was hard to tell the difference.

4

AVERY

Sergeant Lincoln Asher was back.

It was Sunday night, cold and windy, and most of the other readers had already packed up for the evening.

You should have too.

Yeah, clearly, I'd missed the memo.

Dressed in navy-blue slacks, just like last night, and the same jacket over his baby-blue NOPD uniform shirt, he covered the short distance between Pirate's Alley, nestled alongside St. Louis Cathedral, and my table. Without a word, he pulled out the chair opposite mine and dropped his big body onto it.

The chair's legs squealed under the sudden onslaught of his muscular frame and then quieted, as though understanding that the sergeant was not a man to piss off.

Which was possibly the only reason that I opened my mouth and attempted to do just that: "Still alive?"

His full lips didn't twitch at my snarky jab. "Don't sound so disappointed."

"Trust me, I'm not."

Blue eyes zeroed in on my face. "You're not disappointed that I'm alive?"

My brain pin-wheeled, trying to unravel the riddle of his words. "What? No. I meant that of course I'm disappointed."

"Of course." He drew out his wallet from his jacket and pulled money from the cash pocket. A crisp hundred-dollar bill winked at me just before he pinned Benjamin Franklin to the table with his palm.

"What is that?"

"What's it look like?"

Unease settled in my limbs, as did a ball of disgust. Familiar memories of unknown hands, groping my body awake, boiled deep, and I purposely cut eye contact with him to drink some of my hot chocolate. "I'm not sucking your dick, Sergeant."

Briefly, so briefly I wondered if I'd imagined it, his mouth tightened with displeasure. "Did I ask you to suck my dick?"

My gaze dropped to the money.

"I want you to read my cards," he growled, "the way you did for that woman yesterday."

"You mean, you want me to tell you what you want to hear?" I leaned forward, catching the flash of his blue eyes. "Let me tell you something." I tapped the corner of the Benjamin Franklin, making sure not to touch his hand. "You could put five-hundred bucks on this table, and I *still* wouldn't suck your dick."

That did it.

His features hardened, and my breath caught. Yesterday, he'd been relatively easygoing, halfway engaging. Right now, there was nothing easy about Lincoln Asher. *Callous* was the first word to come to mind. *Cruel* was the next, as though he was a man so deep in hell that he'd not seen sunlight in years.

"If you were any other woman, I'd test that theory of yours."

My back straightened at the punishing note in his voice. "What the hell does that mean?"

"It means that everyone has a price, and I've got no doubt that yours is lower than most." He matched my pose, leaning in, twining Benjamin between his index and middle fingers like the most enticing bite of candy I'd ever seen. "It means," he went on, voice low, "that I followed you home last night and I saw where you lived. I've been in those apartments before, and it's no secret that your living situation isn't exactly high-society living. Five hundred bucks would go a long way for you."

I . . . I—

There was something obviously wrong with me. My fingers trembled and my knees locked together and my breathing sounded erratic even to my own ears, and I was . . . aroused. For the first time in my life, I was turned on, and it figured that after a childhood like mine, a stalker would be the thing to harden my nipples and make me want to set my hand between my legs.

Arrogant prick.

My hands moved over the Thoth deck, shuffling mindlessly.

Put him in his place.

"I carry a gun."

I stifled a groan. Of all the things to threaten a police officer with, *that* was my choice of weapon?

Asher's dark brows lifted. "You ever fire it?"

"Yes." *No.* I had, however, made use of my taser on multiple occasions when the situation called for it.

"At what?"

A hard swallow stuck in my throat. "Wouldn't you like to know?"

His husky laughter rang loud in my ears. "You're a shit liar."

"I wasn't lying."

"Yeah, sure you weren't."

"Do you want me to read your cards or not?"

He fell silent, and for a moment there was nothing but the distant sounds of laughter and screams from Bourbon, mingled with the quiet murmur of Tabby weaving a story of lust and love to her client. I took the reprieve to study him in a way that I hadn't last night—I didn't need to have the Sight to know that Lincoln Asher was a dark, restless soul. His sins were apparent in the jagged scars on his cheek, as well as a split in his bottom lip.

The cold weather, maybe, but more likely that he'd taken a fist to the face recently.

Dropping my gaze to his hands, I noted his bruised knuckles with a silent whistle of appreciation. I had no doubt that Sergeant Lincoln Asher had returned the punch tenfold—aside from the break in his bottom lip, his harsh face was otherwise untouched.

Except for the scars, of course.

Blue eyes seared me when I met his gaze, and those icy depths were as turbulent as the waters swirling in the Mississippi River. "I want to know my future," he said roughly. "My past . . ." An equally rough laugh reverberated in his chest, the sound so devoid of emotion that it might as well have been a gust of wind without a storm. "I don't give a fuck about my past."

I slipped a card from the deck, setting it facedown on the table. "You can't run from the past." I knew that for a fact—

on the rare occasions when I tried to let go of the hate, a trip of fate always had me right back at the start again, staring at Jay Foley's face on some screen and remembering that he'd ripped my world straight from under my feet.

I pulled two more cards and settled them on top of the first—the stack of three would represent the sergeant's heart.

If he even had one.

Card by card I laid out the rest of the spread, all the while wondering why a man like Asher would be so utterly consumed with something so fanciful as tarot readings. Then again, it was human nature to crave the unknown, to be titillated by the notion that with the flick of a wrist and the flash of a card, your destiny could be revealed.

Setting the deck aside, I drew my heavy jacket deeper over my shoulders to ward off the late-night chill. "I can't read your future without acknowledging the past." With my index finger, I gently tapped a selection of cards on the left half of the spread. "You'll find that your reading is uneven, unexplained, and whatever answers you seek will have a bottomless pit." At his silence, I added, "But I can read to you what's in your heart, what it desires most above everything else. Maybe that, combined with your future, will make up for ignoring the rest."

5

LINCOLN

I dipped my chin toward the spread she'd laid out. "That's fine," I said, like my heart actually factored into the equation—as though it had factored into *any* equation during the last thirty-four years. I agreed to what she said as though I gave a fuck about what a set of cards might tell me.

Despite my initial reaction to her reading last night, I firmly believed that free will triumphed over destiny or the fates or whatever the hell people were calling it nowadays. My actions had direct consequences, and on the flip of a dime, I could find myself in a very different situation than I had ten minutes earlier.

The cards weren't why I was here tonight.

No, I was here because of *her*, this unnamed woman who lived in one of the largest homes in the Quarter, though its (alleged) tortured past meant that no one gave a shit that the stories of murdered sultans and flayed human body parts were nothing more than rumored fabrications regurgitated for every tourist who wandered past on a tour.

This woman intrigued me, with the way she'd hugged

the shadows last night, as though unnerved that somebody might be watching.

I'd watched, but like I'd told her, I'd done so to ensure she made it home safe.

Because you suddenly have a heart?

Yeah, not quite. Or rather, not at all. I'd left that son of a bitch behind in my first foster-home stint. I had no use for it, not then and not now either, which was further proof that this hazel-eyed girl had somehow ground herself under my skin.

There was no tangible reason for my sudden fascination with her, but here I was, ready to pay her to tell me my fortune . . . simply because I'd wanted another chance to talk with her.

Silently, I watched as she flipped over the first card—my "heart's innermost desires," she'd said—and sat back in her chair, a little frown tugging down her lips. She adjusted her jacket again, drawing it closed over her chest even though two buttons were missing.

"Odd," she murmured.

I leaned in, chair creaking beneath me, and stole a glance at the card half-hidden under her hand. Red fiery flames peaked out from behind what looked like arrows. "How so?"

"Oppression." With a slight shake of her head, she smoothed her fingers over the card. "It's the Ten of Wands, and—"

"What?"

"Nothing, it's just that I get this card frequently. Always in this exact spot, too."

"Coincidence." Dropping my elbows to the table, I nodded to the cards laid out before us. "It's like Murphy's Law. If you really think that everything that can go wrong

will go wrong, it probably will. You're looking for those idio-
syncrasies that indicate you've called it all out correctly—
that your life is in the shitter." I tapped the card, just to the
side of her hand. "Same goes here. If you're looking for simi-
larities, they'll appear."

Hazel eyes blinked up at me, and in that moment, I
could have sworn she'd taken a read on my rotten soul.

"In the cards, oppression represents a separation from
the spirit." Again, she drew the jacket tighter, like the bite of
the night wind sank deep into her bones. "It's as though
your moral compass has disappeared in favor of cruel force.
You don't recognize yourself anymore, your needs or your
desires—you're blinded to whatever drives you, a slave to an
ulterior motive that destroys everything else in its path."

Jesus.

This time it was my turn to tug on the sleeves of my
jacket—for a different reason entirely. She hid from the
cold, and I hid from the chance that she might notice the
blood stains on the cuffs of my shirt.

The familiar grip of guilt weighted my limbs. All of it—
every death, every fight—all led to one goal. So I guess she
was right; I had become oppressed by my own motives, no
matter how dirty and vengeful they were.

My phone vibrated in my pocket, and with a raised
finger to ask her to wait, I slipped it out from my pants and
checked the incoming message from an unknown 504 area
code number: *Is it done?*

The blood had been washed from my hands, if not from
my clothes, so yeah, it'd been finished. *10-4*, I typed back
and then hit SEND.

A second later, a single word greeted me on the screen:
Good.

My dead heart gave a rare, pitiful thump, which I

ignored. Emotion could get you killed in my line of work. It could end you in a heartbeat, strip away your life in a second.

"Something important?" she asked, drawing my attention back to her face.

I shook my head. "Just work."

Her hazel eyes never left my face. "You like working for the NOPD, then?"

My life would be easier if I'd only ever clocked in for the police department. But the NOPD wasn't responsible for the scars on my face, the split in my lip, the blood on my clothes. I cleared my throat. "I like putting the bad guys in jail."

The look she leveled on me spoke volumes. "I'll be honest, and I might be wrong here, but crime seems just as rampant as it's always been."

Her words only piqued my curiosity. "How old are you?"

"Do you want me to read your cards or not?"

I didn't give a damn about the cards, especially when her selection seemed to only reflect gloom and doom. Ruin. Death. Oppression. Not a hint of rainbows or unicorns in sight. "Do you get a kick out of telling tourists that their lives are about to take a morbid turn?"

Her shoulders lifted with a casual shrug. "It's life. I'm not telling anyone anything they don't already know."

"Tell me your name."

At my abrupt switch in topic, her eyes narrowed and her teeth sank into her bottom lip with a sharp indrawn breath. "Why do you want to know it?"

Because I . . . well, fuck, what could I say? That from the moment I'd walked up to her, I'd felt some sort of unexplainable pull, like we were tethered to the same string . . . just at opposite ends? That beyond the random need I had to strip her of her clothes and to see her eyes darken with lust, I recognized a little of myself in her?

I'd made a life out of lying and thieving.

I'd dug myself out of hell only to realize that I'd never be able to shake off the embers.

That the darkness which ran through my blood, as cliché as the saying goes, never calmed or fled, but for a reason I couldn't pinpoint, I felt as though this girl could take it. She could handle my shadows, if not the pure darkness.

Never had I craved someone more.

"It's Avery." My gaze jerked up to her face, and she tilted her chin up defiantly, daring me to question her. "My name is Avery Washington."

I rolled her name over my tongue silently; imagined whispering it against her neck as I plunged into her body; recited it two more times with the fantasy of her on her knees, her lips closing around my cock.

She was a shit liar.

To anyone else, her defiantly raised chin and the challenge in her eyes would have left them feeling as though she'd uttered the truth. But I read liars for a living—hell, *I* was a liar, and I recognized the twitches in her façade for what they were.

I settled back, observing the way she pressed her feminine fingers to the base of her neck and swallowed. "You from N'Orleans?" I asked, wondering if she'd lie about that too.

She met my gaze head-on. "Born and raised."

"Same here."

She didn't roll her eyes but I had the feeling that she wanted to. "I figured."

"Yeah?"

With a short nod, Avery flipped the cards over on the table. "You may meet a lot of different people, Sergeant, but so do I. Everything about you screams this city, starting with the jaded twinkle in your eye."

I laughed hard at that, the sound entirely foreign and rusty to my ears. I never smiled. I never laughed. But, damn it if she didn't make me want to start practicing. "A jaded twinkle?"

Shifting in her chair, Avery muttered something beneath her breath. Then, louder, "It's the color blue of your eyes."

Heat spiked south of my belt at her admission. When I spoke, there was no mistaking the husk in my voice. "Did you spend last night thinking about the color of my eyes, Avery?"

"*What*? Absolutely not."

I stretched out one arm, making no effort to conceal the way I set my hand next to hers. Tan to pale, large against small. She was tiny compared to me, and even that was enticing. My thumb crossed over her pinky, and I stifled a satisfied purr when she flexed her hand . . . and kept her hand right next to mine. "I'd be all too happy—"

"Avery." Jerking toward the sound of the unknown voice, I noticed that the reader one table over had stood up and crossed over to stand beside Avery. The stranger's eyes zeroed in on me, unwavering. "I'm going to pack everything up for the night and I suggest that you do the same."

Her hand slipped away.

"You're right," Avery said, her tone more tepid than I'd heard from her yet. She spared me a quick glance. "It's late, Sergeant Asher, and it's obvious that you haven't come back tonight to learn about your future."

Apparently, she'd sussed me out just as I'd done to her.

I rose from my chair and folded it. "It's obvious," I

drawled, using her words, "that you don't care for the bullshit."

"I don't."

Succinct as her tone was, I spotted a blush crest her cheeks. "Then, no bullshit." When she set her backpack on the table to unzip, I closed in, stepping up close so that she was forced to look up at me. Only when we locked eyes did I speak in a tone low enough that the words were clearly intended only for her and not for her friend. "I spent last night wondering about that smart mouth of yours—how you'll taste or what noises you might make when I drive you to come on my tongue."

I waited, not moving, for her to reply.

She didn't disappoint.

Her tongue swiped out along her plush lower lip. "I don't date."

"No one said anything about dating."

White teeth bit her lip, and those hazel eyes of hers flashed fire and unmistakable want. "I don't fuck."

That word coming off her lips was like a calling card to my dick. She might not *fuck* now but she would, dirty and raw and so damn good that she'd carve her territory into my back with her nails. "If you don't," I drawled, "that just means you haven't done it right."

Her jaw snapped shut, molars cracking together. Her cheeks burned red. "I wouldn't . . ." She swallowed, then ducked her head to continue packing up. "You couldn't handle someone like me, Sergeant—"

"Lincoln."

"What?"

"Call me Lincoln," I repeated, fully aware of the fact that I wanted Avery Washington like nothing I'd ever wanted in my life—outside of one thing. "Lincoln," I said again, "not sergeant."

"As I was saying, *Asher*"—the challenge in her eyes lit my own to see her flat on her back with that same damn fire goading me on—"you couldn't handle me. You think you could, but you can't. Now, if you'll excuse me, I have places to be." She shrugged into her backpack and then bundled up the chairs under one arm. The table, she glared at, and then stepped away. "Don't follow me tonight or I'll call the cops on you."

Her threat stole more rusty laughter from me. "I'm sure my guys will enjoy the chance to cuff me."

"Someone has to," she said, "and it will never be me."

With that, she turned away and ducked down Pirate's Alley. The shadows of St. Louis Cathedral enclosed her within their depths like a physical door being clamped shut behind her.

Locking me out.

"Stay away from her, Sergeant Asher."

I glanced over at Avery's friend, refusing to show her even an ounce of the desire Avery sparked within me. Inclining my head in a short nod, I stepped back. "Have a good night, ma'am."

"I've heard about you, you know—we all have."

"My condolences."

She approached, and it was in that moment that I spotted the tattoo on her right temple. It was small and round, like a stamp made for deceit. She'd been marked by the devil himself. "You kill without guilt, destroy lives without impunity. You act"—she dropped her voice to a rough pitch—"like you are the executioner and the jury, all in the name of what? Money? Conceit?"

If money were a motivator, I would have moved far from

New Orleans years ago. But I didn't owe this woman a damn thing, and so I gave her a small salute and then turned on my heel.

She could hate me for what I'd done—I didn't care one way or the other—but the tattoo on her face was a direct indication that she was no better than me—even if she'd left that life behind. She'd fucked; I'd killed. At the end of the day, when the result was exactly the same, we were equals.

I knew that for a fact; I'd been marked with that same tattoo the day I'd turned sixteen.

6

AVERY

B etween my legs, my core pulsed.

It sounded ridiculous, *so* ridiculous, and yet as I stepped up to the register at my local corner store, it was all I could think about.

Damn you, Asher.

The cash drawer clanged shut. "Just the bottle of wine tonight, Avery?"

When you went to the same corner store five days per week for odds and ends—for *years*—you tended to build up a camaraderie with the staff. "Just the wine, Pete." Feeling my cheeks redden, I adjusted my backpack. I'd dropped everything else off at home before deciding that wine was in order because I couldn't, no matter how hard I tried, pretend that Asher hadn't flipped the script on me. "Just been a long day."

Pete, one half of the duo who owned and operated Flambeaux, nodded and passed over my change. "Try running a twenty-four-hour convenience store, baby." His tone was dry, but the smile on his face remained open and friendly.

"You ever decide to quit with the cards, Salvatore and I could use an extra hand."

Pete and his husband, Sal, had been trying to recruit me for years now. Back when I'd been a teenager, I'd considered it. Discounts on food, two bosses who were so damn kind it was almost unreal—and it didn't hurt that they both knew I was a runner, and thus put up with the name changes without even a blink of the eye. But always the fear lingered that one of my stepfather's cronies would wander in and I'd be screwed.

Or that Pete and his husband would discover my real identity.

Jackson Square lent me its shadows and tourists; Flambeaux could ruin everything with its fluorescent lights and steady stream of French Quarter residents.

"You push a hard bargain," I murmured, dropping my wallet into my backpack and pressing the merlot bottle to my chest. "If I had any good sense . . ."

The bell over the front door chimed with a newcomer, and Pete called out a hello. To me, he said, "If you had any good sense you'd ditch the tarot gig or at least take up with one of the local fortune-reading businesses in the area. Sal and I worry about you out there. People are idiots."

I offered the wine up in silent salute. "People are *definitely* idiots."

Pete slowly shook his head, even as he let out a sigh in clear disappointment. "Stick to Bourbon on your walk home, baby girl. Text me when you get there."

Twenty-five years old or not, I'd still be a kid in Pete's eyes until I was wrinkled and gray. After a quick hug goodbye, I stepped outside with the wine in hand. I didn't drink often because I hated losing control over my body, but tonight . . . I briefly squeezed my eyes shut.

Tonight, I'd discovered my first taste of lust and, honestly, I wasn't a fan.

Once upon a time, in a far, far away land, when I'd first found myself alone and scared, I'd pictured my savior. Chalk it up to a youth spent devouring Disney films, but I'd absolutely imagined my Prince Charming as the requisite blond with the blue eyes and the tall physique—to say nothing of the fact that he'd be sweet and gentlemanly and oh-so-handsome.

If it was a test to see if he measured up to a girl's youthful dreams, Lincoln Asher failed on every front—aside from his Haint blue eyes.

Maybe he's the sort of man you crave now.

I wouldn't know.

From the first time I'd awoken on my cot at the homeless shelter to find a strange man's hand between my legs, I'd refused to entertain even the possibility of dating or fucking.

Until now. Until Lincoln Asher had given me a glimpse of what he could offer to ensure that I came screaming the way Katie had last night.

Kicking a stray glass bottle out of my way, I strolled down quiet St. Phillip Street toward Bourbon. On either side of me, nineteenth-century properties sprung up like vibrantly hued doll houses. At this time of day, their cheery vibe took a backseat for a more haunting quality. Sparse lights lined the street, and up ahead a group of teenagers formed a tight circle, their voices pitching loudly into the still night.

"Look how pretty she is," one guy drawled, his voice a little garbled since his back was to me. "Her hair is so shiny."

"So shiny," his buddy echoed. He slung an arm around his friend's shoulders, leaning forward as though to inspect something on the ground.

I waited for the bark of a dog or a mewl of a feral cat. On more than a few occasions, I'd taken strays in. While the Quarter's stray cat population numbers in the hundreds, dogs weren't that far behind in numbers. My apartment building allowed animals, and I'd registered Katie and myself with the local LSPCA as a foster home for animals.

Maybe it was a downfall of mine, but I couldn't bear to see a living creature relegated to the streets. It just wasn't in me.

My pace hastened as I approached the group, fingers tight around the wine bottle because you never really knew. But if they were messing with a stray, then there wasn't a chance in hell I'd let them carry on and hurt the poor thing.

"Hey."

No one turned at my greeting.

"Hey!"

The two closest whipped around, their faces cast in shadows. Now that I was close, I noted that they were college-aged. Bigger bodies, broader shoulders. Worry pierced me, and I shoved it aside recklessly.

"What the fuck do you want?" the one with brown hair snapped.

Don't be Laurel. Don't cower. Don't run.

"I thought I heard y'all messing with a dog. Came to see if maybe you'd like for me to take her off your hands."

Good, that was good.

"You hear that?" He punched his red-headed friend in the arm. "This chick wants to take the dog off our hands."

Red hitched a laugh that reminded me of dark alleyways and lost souls. "If only we had a collar for her."

"Right? A collar and a leash"—he looked to me, chin dipping as his gaze no doubt skimmed down my body—"so we could let you take her home."

Were all college boys idiots? These ones had clearly wandered down here from Uptown, near the universities. Their preppy clothes screamed *privilege*. If the street were more lit, I had no doubt that I'd spot red eyes and haggard features. Boys like them came down to the Quarter for their latest fix, which generally came in the form of little white lines of powder.

"Don't need a leash or a collar." Swinging my backpack to my front, I made sure to keep my eyes on the idiots as I unzipped the bag and searched for the spare leash I always kept on hand, just in case. The wine bottle I tucked under my left armpit. "Let me take the dog and you can go back to the bars."

Red laughed again. "What do you say, boys? Should we give her the dog?"

He stepped to the side and my stomach bottomed out.

In the center of their circle was a girl on her knees. Jeans torn, shirt ripped, hair a tangled mess down the length of her back. She hugged herself around the middle as though she'd never know kindness from another human being again, and I didn't have to look at her face to know that the whimper of sorrow echoing in my ears belonged to her.

Mother. Fuckers.

"Step away from her." All too familiar memories clouded my vision and I thrust them away. "Step the fuck back from her."

Another whimper, this one so keening that she actually sounded like an abused pup.

"How about we take you, too?" Red's grasping hands found my backpack and tugged me forward in a hard pull. *Don't cower. Don't run. Don't be Laurel.*

I fell to my knees beside the girl, my shoulder crashing into hers.

Shoving his face close, Red's breath wafted over my face like a harbinger of death by cigarettes and booze. "How about we take that leash out of your hands and tie you up? How about that, boys?" He glanced away at his friends, teeth shining off-white as he grinned. "You think we should walk her down Bourbon like the bitch she—"

The wine bottle shattered over his head.

Silence pervaded our circle, aside from the girl's crying, as Red dropped to the cracked sidewalk with a heavy *thump*.

And then everyone shifted into motion.

"Jesus fucking Christ!"

"Get the bitch!"

They launched toward me as my hands peeled open my backpack in frantic motions, diving for the taser I always kept hidden in the front pocket. Only problem was, the electric-prongs were a one-shot only type of deal. And while I had my gun in the bag, too, I'd lied to Sergeant Asher about something else.

I'd never fired it, not a single time.

Pete had given it to me a few years back for safety. We'd always talked about going to the range, but life had gotten busy for him. Which meant that I owned a gun I didn't even know how to use, aside from a general knowledge to pull the trigger and hope for the best.

Fan-flipping-tastic.

Large hands went to my shoulders, dragging me away from my backpack, away from my gun, away from the girl who needed saving. Her wide eyes followed me as I let my body go lax, the backs of my legs scraping raw along the unforgiving cement.

Don't fight. Wait.

I held onto my breath until my captor released me with the order to "get down, bitch."

I was a great order-follower when I wanted to be.

I leaned back against the sidewalk just as he said, then wrapped my hand around the base of my taser where I'd quickly stashed it in my jacket pocket.

He didn't see it coming.

I aimed the taser at his crotch.

Pulled the trigger.

The two electrode prongs released, zooming straight for ground zero, and I curled and rolled to the side to avoid his massive body landing on mine.

Satisfaction flared at the sight of him cupping his dick, eyes rolling to the back of his head.

"Asshole," I ground out before hopping to my feet, not a little wearily. There were three more of them and only one of me, and as bad as I was at math, the odds were certainly not in my favor.

The sound of bone crunching had me whirling around to see Lincoln Asher grab Brown Hair by the shirt collar and deliver a punch straight to his face. Another crack, this time the man's nose splintering. Blood burst like a fountain, which didn't stop Asher. He reeled back and clocked the guy yet again, his knuckles glistening under the dim lighting.

My stomach heaved.

Don't think about blood and Momma and death. Focus, focus, focus.

Scuffling shoes across the cement teased me back to reality, and I turned just in time to see one of the guys come at me from the side. He went for my hair, chubby fingers grasping at the long strands, ugly words crossing his lips. I jabbed my taser into his rib cage, thankful for the stun-gun feature when his brows lifted in shock and he mumbled something incoherent under his breath.

He stumbled, one foot crossing over the other like a

drunken sailor, hand outreached for the stucco wall of the house beside us. His fingers barely grazed it before he went down, hard.

Thank God.

"Done this before?"

I wouldn't have thought I'd find Asher's raspy voice comforting, but I suppose that was before I'd been jumped by four boys who thought their dicks were the equivalent to a unicorn's horn.

Asher had the last guy on the ground, belly flat on the sidewalk, as he handcuffed the guy's hands behind his back.

"Not a single time," I muttered, then turned my attention to the girl. At the sound of my shoes crunching over gravel, her shoulders visibly jerked. I knelt beside her, careful to leave space between us so she didn't feel threatened. "Are you okay?"

Her bottom lip quivered and she ducked her head. "I-I . . ."

I understood her fear. I'd breathed it, I'd been reborn to it.

Like she was a terrified colt, I parked my butt on the cement and settled my hands on my knees so she could keep watch on where they were at all times. With a tilt of my chin, I said, "That's Sergeant Asher. He's with the New Orleans Police Department, and I can guarantee you're safe with him." Hadn't he said that he found no thrill in pursuing those who couldn't protect themselves? "My name is Avery."

She swallowed and then gave a little nod. "Casey. Thank you . . . thank you for stepping in."

It hurt to know that she'd expected me to walk on by, even when I'd thought she was a dog. It indicated that others had; they'd put down their heads and continued on with their night even as she'd been assaulted.

Shrugging out of my jacket, I held it out to her. "Take this."

"You'll be cold."

I offered her a small smile. "I've dealt with worse. Take it."

When she did, Asher stepped forward, his face menacing and dark and unholy—but he'd saved Casey and me both. "Ma'am, you'll need to go to the district station over on Royal." As if sensing the girl's hesitation, he put up his hands, palms facing out. "I know you don't want to. I know it's going to be hard to explain what happened and relive it, but a statement from you will ensure these guys go to jail, you hear me?"

"I hear you."

Asher gave a clipped nod. "Good. Now, you can wait until backup arrives, so they can transport these guys to lockup and I can take you—it might be a minute. Or maybe Avery wouldn't mind walking you over to the station. Your choice."

What? *No.*

In no universe was it a good idea for me to bring Casey to the Eighth District Police Station—not because I didn't care to see her safely there. I did, really. But bringing her would be like walking into the lion's den.

I swallowed thickly as youthful fears set in like prongs latching onto my skin.

It would be just my luck to run into someone who recognized me.

Red emitted a groan as he tried to roll onto his back and then realized his bound hands limited his mobility. "Uncuff me, man," he groaned. "Fuck me."

Asher shot him a look of disdain. "You're not anyone's type, kid. But your wish might be granted with where you're going."

Casey's eyes went wide, and she shuffled behind me. "Can we go?" she whispered. "I don't want . . ." She licked her lips, clearly nervous. "I don't want to stay here."

It was on the tip of my tongue to tell her no.

I tried but the words wouldn't come. With a sigh, I grabbed my backpack by the strap and hooked it over my right shoulder. My taser went into the front pocket of my bag, just in case.

"Thank you." Casey wrapped her arms around her middle. "Just . . . thank you."

Her quiet praise didn't sit well with me. It felt too much like a spotlight, bright and without a single place to hide. I averted my gaze from the gratitude lining her bruised features. "Don't worry about it. Let's go."

I didn't make it two steps past Asher before his large hand clamped down on my forearm, stilling my escape. He'd touched me twice tonight; the first, a simple brushing of our fingers, had stolen my breath. This time, my heart thudded in my chest with something that felt a lot like antic- ipation.

"Have a problem, Sergeant?" I kept my tone light, slightly wry, but I worried he could detect what I so wanted to hide. Interest, in him. It was incredibly inconvenient.

His thumb stroked my arm. "Don't leave the station without me."

"Is that a request or an order?"

I felt his breath by my ear, rustling the strands of my hair. "An order, Miss Washington." His thumb continued its up and down strokes, sending sparks of *something* throughout my body. "You good at obeying?"

There was no mistaking the way his voice dropped an octave. This man was not one for bullshit, as he'd told me, and so I wouldn't give him any in return.

With a little tug, I pulled free of his grasp and flashed him a grin. "Not in the least. Obeying has never been one of my strong suits."

"Start learning," he growled in what I had to assume was the tone he took with the men and women in his unit. "I'll see you at the station. Don't make me chase you."

The words had the opposite effect on me than what he'd probably hoped.

They didn't inspire fear.

No, they inspired lust.

Sergeant Lincoln Asher could chase me all he wanted, but unless I let him, he'd never catch me.

7

AVERY

The back of my neck prickled with anticipation as I waited on Asher by the eighth district precinct. It would be all too easy to blame the goosebumps flaring to life on my skin on the cool, wrought-iron fence against my back. A lot easier than admitting the truth, which was—

"You followed a command, Miss Washington. I'm impressed."

My gaze cut to his powerful form striding toward me from Royal Street. The dim street lights allowed the darkness to hug him, casting shadows across his face. His left hand rested on the butt of the gun on his hip, and I swallowed that inconvenient anticipation all over again. Pushed it as far down as it would go until it'd been strangled into nonexistence.

I didn't have time for men, not even ones who looked like, or exuded the confidence that Lincoln Asher did.

Tilting my chin, I allowed my crossed arms to fall to my sides as I pushed away from the fence. "I thought I'd show you how it's done, considering you followed me when I specifically told you not to."

Nothing in his stoic expression hinted at humor, but I had the impression that he was laughing at me. "We can pretend that's what went down."

"Pretend?" My nose wrinkled as I kept my eyes on his face. He stopped less than a foot away, looming large in front of me. His close proximity forced me to tip my head back to maintain eye contact. Lincoln Asher was a big man—a lot bigger than me.

"Pretend," he confirmed evenly. "I was on my way home for the night when my radio went off with a 103-F." He cupped my elbow and, for a half-second, I was convinced he was about to pull me into his embrace. My mind raced with the possibilities, shifting through them each individually— would he kiss me? Did he want to? Hell, did *I* want him to?

Then his words actually penetrated the thick fog of that unwanted anticipation, and I blinked at the unfamiliar term. "103-F?"

"A fight."

Asher didn't pull me into a hug. Instead, he backed me up, using his much larger frame to intimidate me into stepping backward, toward the pale-yellow district station that looked a lot more like an elegant English mansion than a home base for cops.

My feet followed his lead, regardless of the fact that I had no plans to step back inside the building with him. "So what, you thought you'd come and rescue me?" My voice stuck in my throat, and I forced a rough cough to clear it. "You're assuming I needed your help."

Blue eyes flashed in my direction. "You're assuming that I even knew it was you."

Good point.

Embarrassment slithered like vines around my legs, dragging my pace to a slow crawl.

He mimicked my pause, his heavy combat boots grinding to a halt, his wide shoulders turning so that we were chest to chest. Or, more accurately, chin to chest. His fingers fluttered up my arm, coasting over my right shoulder. Landing directly on that sensitive place where my neck and shoulder met. Stealing my breath and infusing my head with wild, foreign fantasies that were as alien to me as the man invading my space.

"I had no idea it was you, but the moment I did . . ." His thumb arched upward, sweeping under the jut of my jaw in a gesture that was both erotic and possessive. "I don't get angry, Avery. I never lose my cool. And then I saw you hit the pavement, and I was ready to unload my clip into any fucker who touched you. *No one* touches you or they answer to me."

At my swallow, I felt the imprint of his thumb like a stamp on my neck. "You hardly know me."

His blue eyes fell to my lips. "No, I don't. Not yet, but I will."

With that mysterious comment, he stepped back, and the sudden space was like I'd been relieved from a vacuum. My lungs seized air in one, two, three quick breaths. Desperate to change the conversation, I averted my face and watched a group of tourists stumble down Royal with green Hand Grenade bottles clutched in their hands.

"You want me to give a statement, don't you?" I asked, my gaze locked on the tipsy tourists. "That's why you asked me to stick around?"

"In part."

"And the other part?"

It happened then, just the smallest uptick of his mouth. It was hardly a smile. Hardly worth noting at all, really. But still, I felt it all the way down to my toes. Felt it all the more when Asher tucked a hand against the small of my back and murmured, "Don't ask questions when you aren't ready for the answers."

Did I want to push for more?

Pushing meant admitting to this unwanted attraction, an attraction like I'd never felt before.

But pushing also meant gaining something in return—information, for one. Lincoln Asher carried himself like he held the weight of the world on his shoulders. It seemed unlikely that he could get to where he was now within the NOPD without learning a thing or two about the city's ring of politicians. I wanted access to those secrets. I needed access to that information.

I craved, after all these years, to set aside my thirst for revenge and live my life without glancing over my shoulder every other moment.

More than anything, I wanted to know the reason why my stepfather had my mother murdered in cold blood. A former oil tycoon like him, Foley had swept her death under the rug with hand-rolled cash to all the right people, I had no doubt about that. And that wasn't even covering the fact that he'd wanted me dead, too.

Mentally shaking loose the memories, I indicated the station with my hand. "Should we go in? I'd rather not spend my entire night on the front steps."

My abrupt change of heart earned me a hard, unrelenting once-over.

Asher didn't say a word as he spun on his heel and took the steps two at a time. I followed at a brisk pace, head held high. It was time for me to stop hiding in the shadows, however terrifying the prospect.

Pulse racing as we entered the marble-floored foyer, I glanced around the brightly lit room. Receptionist desk to my right. A hallway extending away from the lobby, leading to god-knows-where.

"Follow me."

At the sharp note in Asher's voice, I drew my jacket tight around my shoulders.

This is what I'd wanted all these years—an in. A chance to learn more about my stepfather. An opportunity to do more than just passively collect information from those who sat at my table to have their tarot cards read.

Not that I expected the mayor of New Orleans to be strolling around a police precinct on a Sunday night, but the mere possibility had me stretching on my toes and craning my neck, just in case.

"This is us," Asher murmured as he paused by a wooden door to our right. He palmed it open and ushered me inside with a hand to the center of my back. Desks were haphazardly arranged throughout the room. Some had computers on them. Others were bare, save for stacks of papers. A lone officer sat on the far end of the room, shoulders slouched as he stared at the computer screen before him. Asher indicated to a desk to our left, and he settled his hand on the worn wood. "Take a seat here. I need to grab something first, and then we'll get this over with."

I met his gaze. "Not even a little scared that I'll take off?"

Asher glanced at the other officer, and then retrained his attention on me. "You aren't going anywhere."

"You're cocky."

"No," he said with another one of his barely-there smirks, "I'm just confident that you're craving something else entirely from me, and I plan to deliver until you're weak in the knees and sprawled across my lap." The grin that widened his mouth was all male satisfaction. "Get comfortable."

The expanse of his back winked at me as he slipped through the open door and out into the hall.

It took a whopping two seconds for the bravado to un-pinch from my features.

I dropped inelegantly to the rolling desk chair, my knees —true to form—trembling way too hard to keep me upright or my dignity intact. Lincoln Asher was . . . he was—I skipped my sweaty palms across my thighs and drew in a sharp breath.

He was trouble with a capital T.

Trouble for my piece of mind, for my aims, for my body. Even now, I couldn't forget the way his hand had felt curled around my neck. The rapid tattoo of my heart rate had yet to slow, and as I sat there, there was only one lingering thought: *I wanted more*.

I was twenty-five, a virgin, and the only man who'd ever kissed me had taken that desire from me with a disturbing thrust of his tongue in my mouth and his fingers yanking painfully on my hair. I'd sworn then that I would never give another man the opportunity to take what wasn't his.

I bowed to no one.

And yet, in the span of two days, Asher had thrown everything I wanted to believe about myself out the window —and he'd done it all with nothing more than the timbre of his voice, the rawness in his blue eyes, and a touch that was impossibly seductive.

"Stop," I muttered beneath my breath.

Here I was sitting at his desk, and instead of making use of my time, I was acting like a lovesick idiot. *Get your mind back in the game.*

Casting a quick glance at the other officer, whose head

was bobbing as though he'd passed out at his desk, I drew my attention back to Asher's workspace. Papers were stacked orderly in manila folders. Post-it sticky notes lined the right edge of the desk—across them all, he'd scrawled phone numbers and names of people I didn't know.

As quietly as possible, I tried each desk drawer.

The bottom one was filled with nothing but excess computer paper and empty envelopes.

The chair across the room screeched back when I tugged on the second drawer's handle, and I dropped my hand like I'd personally picked up a ball of flames. Clutched the lip of the desk as though I hadn't just been snooping.

"You good?" the officer asked, strolling toward me. He had bloated features and an equally round gut. Something told me he rarely worked the streets anymore. He nodded toward his desk. "Can't believe I fell asleep."

My fingers dug into the wood. "I noticed." I forced a casual smile. *Act normal.* "Long shift?"

His mouth melted into a grimace. "Didn't even realize I slept straight through the end of it."

"Ouch."

"Yeah." He cocked his head to the side. "You Asher's girl?"

"What?"

"You dating Asher? He doesn't bring anyone in here, ever. Straight to the interview rooms for civilians." He paused and let his dark eyes rove over my face. "It's protocol. Not bringing non-personnel in here, I mean."

Palms turning slick, I shifted in the rolling chair. My heels dug into the ground, and I pulled myself forward. Hands moving forward, glossing under the desk until . . . My index finger brushed against cool metal. It felt like a latch, and one trace of it with my fingers proved that accurate. But it wasn't—no, there was no way.

"Ma'am?"

My spine stiffened with the effort to not jolt at the sound of the officer's voice. "We're, umm . . ." *Think!* "We're old friends. We go way back." *To, like, yesterday.* I pushed down on the latch and sent up a silent prayer that I hadn't just doomed myself. "I'm not his girl."

Dark eyes didn't move from my face. "Then why did he say he was about to put you over his lap?"

The second drawer, the one I'd wanted to open earlier, popped open. It extended no farther than an inch, maybe two, but holy crap, this was the moment. I tore my eyes away from the drawer and tried to look normal.

Act normal.

My heart, meanwhile, thundered in my chest like a stampede of elephants dancing on already-fractured ice.

"It's an old joke," I told the officer with a smooth smile. The same smile I used on my customers in Jackson Square. "Ash—*Lincoln,* he's had a crush on me for years."

The guy's nose wrinkled as he shifted his gaze downward, over the top half of my body—which was all that was visible to him above the desk. "How old are you?"

Clearly, not old enough. "Thirty." I lied, smiling wider, toothier, faker. "I've got a baby face. It's the curse of all women in my family."

His answer was nothing more than an incomprehensible mumble.

"What was that?" I itched to pop open the drawer fully. Patience was both my strongest suit and my biggest weakness. I was complicated like that. "I'm sorry, I didn't catch what you said."

Digging into his back pocket, he pulled out his wallet

and flipped it open. Five steps brought him to the far corner of the desk, and then he was palming a rectangular white card and sliding it over to me.

I picked it up, turned it over, and stared at the name printed in small, block font across the back: DT. SAMUEL LOCKAR. "Thank you?"

"In case you need anything." He rapped his knuckles against the desk. "Lying won't get you anywhere, miss."

It was a struggle to swallow the sudden lump in my throat. "I didn't lie." Twenty-five to thirty was more like a dramatization, if anything.

"Yeah." The detective didn't sound like he believed me. "Let's put it this way. Asher's known to like 'em younger. Just think about that before you keep up y'all's . . . friendship."

Lockar didn't give me a chance to say anything else. He swept out of the office, gently shutting the door behind him. Leaving my breath somewhere over the Mississippi River because it surely wasn't with me right now.

What in the hell did he mean? Asher liked them *younger*?

I caught my wide-eyed expression in the black screen of the desktop computer. There was no way Lockar could mean . . . . I lifted my hand to trace my reflection in the screen. No way. I hadn't gotten that sort of vibe from Asher at all.

And what do you really know about men?

Fuck.

I turned sharply from the computer and got down to business. This was not an opportunity I was going to lose out on. Snapping open the drawer, I gave the interior a cursory glance. Restaurant menus littered the space. I dove in a hand, shuffling through the folded pamphlets.

At the sound of a door slamming shut, my shoulders twitched and I held still.

My lungs seized a fistful of air I didn't dare let out, and when three seconds passed with no one waltzing into *this* office, I went back to work.

There had to be something.

Why have a locked drawer if all you kept inside were takeout menus?

On a whim, I tried the other drawers again. They all popped open without trouble, which meant . . . Option Number Two it was, then. No way would a man like Lincoln Asher waste a drawer with a lock. I refused to believe it.

I shoved the menus aside, and if it weren't for the fact that I was searching hard, I never would have noticed it.

Pressed up against the outer edge of the drawer, its cardboard backing facing me, a small, thin notepad caught my eye.

Among restaurant menus and receipts, it stuck out like a jaguar in an aquarium.

I flipped it over.

Names were scrawled down half its length, taking up perhaps four or five lines of the white-lined paper. There was no header at the top. Nothing to signify who these people were or why Asher had taken the time to document them all, and then shove it to where it wouldn't be noticed. I skimmed the names, one by one, my heart hammering in my chest at the mere possibility that Asher might push open the door and catch me.

Josef Banterelli.

Ba-dump.

Micah Welsh.

Ba-dump.

Tom Townsend.

Ba-dump.

Zak Benson.

Ba-dump.

A familiar name on the last line stopped me cold.

Tabitha Thibadeaux.

And then, with a pained whine of dry hinges, the door swung open.

8

AVERY

Asher kicked the door shut with his heel.

Under his right arm, he carried a set of folders—all of which he dropped on the desk, just beside my elbow. "Sorry you had to wait," he said. "I had to pick up Casey's report, and then one of my guys had a question." He glanced up from the folders, in my direction. "You'd think they've never gone through Academy with some of the shit they like to bring to me."

My smile was tight, and I was surprised I could even hear him over the persistent ringing in my ears. The metal rings of his notebook stabbed me in the butt as I shifted uncomfortably in the office chair. Was sitting on the notebook particularly savvy? Not even a little bit. But there'd been little time to do anything else, even unzip my backpack and thrust the notebook inside.

"I always thought that there are no stupid questions."

Taking the seat opposite mine, Asher flipped open the top file. "There are stupid questions. The only people who say there aren't have got too much heart."

An interesting response.

I hummed a little in my throat, deliberating on my answer. There was no mistaking the way his blue eyes flashed hot at the noise, nor the way his fingers tightened around the pen he'd picked up in his left hand. Did I affect him the same way he did to me? I made the noise again, just to test him, and Asher didn't disappoint. His gaze dropped to my mouth, his jaw visibly tightening as though he wanted nothing more than to throw the desk against the wall and sit me on his lap.

The look on Asher's face . . . it was of a man restrained. My thighs clenched together at the realization, and I pinched my knee beneath the desk to break the spell of desire heating my core and curling my toes. It wasn't why I was here.

Liar.

"Are you suggesting that you don't have a heart?" I finally asked, leaning forward to prop my elbows on the desk. The notebook's spiral rings went flat under my weight. *Aw, crap.* Swallowing, I added, "You don't strike me as the cliché type, Sergeant."

He cleared his throat. "Cliché?"

"Yeah." I mimicked him, clearing my throat and dropping my voice by at least an octave. "Hello, I'm Lincoln Asher and you know what's different about me? I'm heartless." I watched his lips twitch, barely skimming the surface of a true smile but coming pretty damn close. "Fun fact," I said in my normal pitch, "the only people who go around saying they're lacking a heart are generally the folks who have actually got *too* much of one, but don't want people to know they're an inner softie."

"You got stats to back you up on this theory?" He set the pen down and met my gaze head-on. "Or are you just theorizin'?"

I offered a smile. "I've lived in the Quarter for over ten years. I know my fair share of heartless assholes."

"And I don't fit the mold?" He sounded pleasantly intrigued by the prospect. "And here I've been thinking all these years that I'm king of the heartless assholes around here. I'm a little ticked off that someone took my crown."

His response made me choke out a surprised laugh. "Was that a joke?"

"What?" Dark brows rose high on his forehead. "Heartless assholes can't be funny?"

"Not the king."

"Ah," Asher murmured, "but we've already agreed that I've been dethroned."

He sure fit the mold for dethroned royalty. Messy hair, bright blue eyes that shone like topaz gems, and those scars that carved the side of his face. Something in his tone intrigued me more than even the scar. Leaning back in my chair, I gave him a slow once-over. "Looking at you, I'd be inclined to think of you as less like a king and more like the king's executioner."

If I weren't studying him so acutely, I would have missed it—the smallest flare of his nostrils and the slight pull of his mouth into a harder, more uncompromising line.

Interesting.

Asher dropped his gaze to the folders before him. "Let's get this done."

For the next twenty or so minutes, he put me through the test.

Where were you walking when you stumbled upon the assault? Back to my apartment.

Did you utilize your stun gun before or after the perpetrator laid hands on you? After.

Did you recognize any of the perps as someone you may have had contact with before tonight? No, they were complete strangers.

With each new question, my hands grew damp and my stomach roiled at the memories. Memories of a younger me, a more innocent me—of groping hands and rickety beds that squeaked under heavy weights.

I'd always been resourceful, even at the age of thirteen when I'd found myself living on the streets with nowhere to go. And there's something to be said about open-ended possibilities.

At any time, I could have filched a ticket for the Mega-Bus, Destination Unknown.

I used to sit by the bus stop, over on Elysian Fields and North Claiborne, with a fried chicken-wing restaurant at my back and concrete all around me. I used to walk there from the French Quarter, at least two miles there and back, and watch people come and go with their colorful suitcases and their laughter catching in the humid, Southern air. At any time, I could have snuck onboard. By the time anyone realized there was a stowaway, like some ruffian-kid out of an old-time movie, we would have been halfway to Alabama or maybe Texas or even Arkansas, depending on which MegaBus I took.

I never did get on that bus.

I never could leave this city, which has gifted me more bad memories than good.

"We're all set."

Hands clenched together in my lap, I put voice to the question burning on my tongue. "Do you like what you do?"

Asher's face gave nothing away, as was the norm for him, I was beginning to see. "Excuse me?"

I nodded to him, and he'd have to be a fool not to realize that I was talking about the noticeable scars across his cheek. He bore his wounds for all to see; mine were secreted away in my heart. But for him, he could leave this job and do something else. I couldn't leave being *me*, no matter how many new names I adopted.

"Do you like being a cop? That's a better way to put it."

Like a veil unraveled by a string, Asher's blue eyes flicked away. "I've been on the job for over a decade."

I'd wondered about his age. Aside from the faint lines that appeared by his eyes when he (rarely) smiled, Lincoln Asher could have been anywhere from mid-twenties to early-forties. But, as a cop, it made sense that he'd blend in.

I've been on the job for over a decade—I turned the words over in my head, pulling them apart and quickly dissecting them. "All right, Mr. Vague." I waggled my brows, teasing him. "You do realize that's not an answer, right? Being on the job and *liking* the job are two completely different things."

Dropping a forearm to the desk, he leaned in. "Reverse the tables. Do you like reading cards out on the Square?"

I could give him the lie or I could give him some semblance of the truth and hope for a smidgeon of it in return. I went for the latter: "It pays the bills." *And gets me much-needed information*. "But, no, it's not a long-term career for me. You won't see me out there in thirty years still catering to folks who refuse to see what's directly in front of them already."

Nothing in Asher's face registered shock, but instinctually, I got the feeling he hadn't expected for me to pull the blunt act. His fingers drummed a monotonous beat on the desk. "Working for the NOPD keeps me focused," he said after a long pause. "If I had the opportunity to do something else, I'd honestly be lost."

"I would be a veterinarian."

Dammit.

Asher's left brow arched high at my unintended confession. "You can't now?"

Not without a high school or a vet degree. Not with a fake name. Not when your stepfather still liked to wax on about his poor dead wife and the stepdaughter who'd turned up dead after killing herself.

"Nah," I murmured, my tone casually dismissive. And then I spun the lie I'd repeated to myself for years now: "It would be fun, but it's hard work. I'm much more suited to reading cards. I can go down to the square whenever I want. There are no rules, no high expectations."

For a moment, he said nothing and the air seemed to shrivel in the silence. Then, "We're all set here . . . unless you've got a question for me about the report?"

My toes curled in my shoes. Right.

"No questions." I hastily stood, then, remembering the spiral-bound notebook on the chair, collapsed back down. "Actually, I have one." My fingers snaked under my butt as Asher watched me from across the desk, his expression all but reading, *Get to it already*. "I'm a little hungry. Maybe it's the adrenaline calming down, I don't know."

Slowly, a smile pulled at his firm mouth. "Are you asking me out to dinner?"

It seems that I am.

Snagging my backpack strap, I drew the bag between my legs and made a show of ducking my head, feigning a bashfulness that wasn't at all me, and drew the zipper tags apart. "Maybe I am." Right butt cheek lifted ever-so-slightly, I pulled the notebook from its place and inched it to home base. Slowly. Slowly. *Slowwwllyyyy*. "It's a little late for dinner but maybe some beignets?" I lifted my chin to peer at him from behind the curtain of my dark hair. "Café du Monde is *so* romantic at this time of night."

For the first time in my life, I fluttered my lashes.

Asher sat back in his chair, his crisp uniform shirt pulling tight across his broad chest. Under the office lights, his NOPD sergeant's badge shined like a beacon of trustworthiness.

The notebook currently dropping into my backpack said otherwise.

Because now that I'd had time to think about it, I recognized the two top names from a recent spread in *The Times-Picayune*. The obituary section, in particular.

Both Josef Banterelli and Micah Welsh were dead.

Slit throats.

Bodies bobbing in the Mississippi River in the early morning hours.

"Beignets it is." Asher flashed me a quick, almost-missed-it grin. "Why don't you wait for me in the hallway? I'll wrap this up and then we can go."

"You got it." I saluted him with fake confidence and hightailed it to the door. The moment I burst free, I pressed my back against the neighboring wall and filled my lungs with oxygen.

It was just a notebook. Nothing more. And yet I felt as though I'd stolen contraband from a drug lord.

Maybe that's because Asher sort of looks *like a drug lord.*

Albeit a sexy one.

With the visual of his shiny fleur-de-lis NOPD badge in the forefront of my mind, I tightened my hold on the strap of my backpack and waited for him to emerge from the office.

A casual sharing of powdered donuts had never hurt anyone, and no matter how touristy the restaurant, Café du Monde had been a local favorite of mine since I was a young girl. Before Momma was brutally murdered and my life upended for reasons I still didn't know.

"Ready to go?"

Like I'd been caught with drugs myself, my butt cheeks clenched together, and my heart went into triple-time as Asher stepped out and then slid the door closed behind him.

"Yup!" The way I popped my *P* was not suspicious at all . . . *not*. I stifled an awkward laugh and tried again. "I'm starved."

Better, that was better.

"For beignets?" He settled a hand on the small of my back, directing me toward a door at the end of the hall with a red-neon EXIT sign posted above it. "I'll be sure to get us two orders."

One shove of his free hand against the steel and we were back out in the Quarter again, music blasting from nearby nightclubs, a hot and humid breeze tangling my hair and whipping it across my face.

I reached up to tug the strands back behind my ears, only Asher beat me to it.

Big, masculine hands framed my face and if I'd been concerned about breathing regularly beforehand, it was nothing compared to now. My lips parted as though on someone else's command and my hair seemed to glue itself to the cushion of my bottom lip.

Asher's hands didn't move, but his blue gaze roved over my face.

Lust.

I wasn't so much of a novice that I didn't recognize the emotion swirling in his eyes, nor the way his body stiffened even as he hunched his shoulders . . . to get closer to my height? It was tough to tell.

"What are you doing?"

Such a stupid question but it formed anyway and found life in the space between us.

"I'm starved," he said, the pads of his thumbs brushing over my jawline with an achingly soft touch. I barely had time to register the fact that it might be the softest caress I'd ever known—at least from my cognitive, adult years—before Asher added, "And not for beignets."

My back collided with the police precinct behind me, my backpack squishing audibly at the abrupt contact, as Asher slid his hands from my face down the length of my arms to where he captured my wrists. He lifted them, and I swore my breathing grew more uneven the higher they were drawn.

Up.

Up.

Up.

Above my head they went, until my wrists were criss-crossed, and he had one hand holding them in place.

Sharply, I inhaled through my nose. I was back in that place again, torn between lifting my knee and nailing him in the balls for manhandling me like I was some throwaway toy and—my eyes squeezed shut at the truth—wanting to see where this led.

My hands jerked at the realization, and Asher only read-justed his grip and dropped his other hand to my collarbone, his fingers teasing at the collar of my shirt.

"What are you doing?" This time when I repeated the question, there was no denying that I sounded like I'd run for miles.

Naturally, Asher sounded completely composed when his firm lips parted to confess, "Kissing you."

This is where you knee him right in the dick. Go on. Do it. Heel up, leg lifted, knee primed in position.

I didn't do any of that.

As if my body had decided to operate on instinct alone, my hips angled to better cradle his weight against my body. It was a total betrayal—I didn't hook up with men and I definitely never gave them the time of day, but Lincoln Asher wasn't like most men.

He was a police sergeant, which meant I had to obey him in some capacity . . . right? Since he was an enforcer of the law, it only made sense that if he set a new rule, it was my duty as an upstanding citizen of New Orleans to see it through to the end.

Sometimes, it felt criminally good to lie to myself.

I tossed my hair back, careful not to smash my head on the stucco behind me. "If you're so hungry," I drawled, trying to gauge the thoughts glittering in his inscrutable blue eyes, "then why haven't you broken your fast yet?"

His grin was lightning-quick.

It was there and then it was gone, and yet I felt warm from its second-long presence anyway.

His grip retightened on my wrists, his gaze never veering from mine. "Oh, I will," he said, his low baritone brimming with silent conviction, "but I think I'll start here first . . ." His fingers tugged at my shirt collar, exposing my neck.

Asher took full advantage.

He lowered his head, kept me pinned to the wall with one hand, and dragged his mouth along my skin.

I trembled under his touch—my limbs, my lips, my damn toes all shaking.

My eyes fell shut and for the first time in my life, I allowed myself to feel.

His broad chest moving against mine as he inhaled deeply.

The soft puffs of air against my skin, with every exhalation, as he gently bit down on my earlobe.

The rough callouses on his palm as they rubbed against my restrained wrists.

Nothing about Lincoln Asher was soft—except, perhaps, for his tongue.

And nothing about my locked position should have been a turn-on, but it was. Oh, it *was*, and when a moan broke free from between my clamped teeth, it was only to hear Asher chuckle softly, like he'd just been given entry to the one place which had always been off-limits.

His lips landed on the underside of my jaw, and I gasped at the contradiction of his roughly-stubbled cheeks as they grated and marked the soft skin of my face.

Another kiss, this one to my cheek.

And then yet another, this one to the corner of my mouth.

It was going to happen.

My fingers curled in expectation and my heart kicked into overdrive and I had a split-moment decision to make: angle my head to receive the kiss or meet him halfway?

I cursed my inexperience.

I cursed my childhood obsession with TV shows that focused more on wildlife in the Rockies than kissing.

I cursed myself for spending hours in the club, waiting while Katie tended the bar, and only imagining what it might be like to be in any pair of feminine shoes while a man worked me into a kissing frenzy.

In the end, I opted for the classic face tilt seen in every rom-com movie ever. Romantic. Unassuming. Patient.

"Open your eyes," came his low order, "I want you to know who's kissing you."

My blinking didn't coincide with a kiss.

Not even a peck.

Instead, a phone's ringtone sliced through the air, angry and loud. Asher's hand fell from my wrists as he stepped back, already reaching into the pocket of his uniform slacks. "Fuck," he ground out, his face a mask I couldn't decipher as he glanced at the name blinking across his screen. "I've got to take this."

"Okay." It was better this way, I told myself. Kissing Sergeant Lincoln Asher was wrong on so many different levels, starting with the fact that he was well-appointed within the NOPD, in a way that made me uncomfortable— and ending with the fact that I didn't particularly *like* him.

Liar.

I shoved the little voice out a window and slammed the proverbial glass shut.

In a voice that I prayed sounded one-hundred percent unaffected, I murmured, "Don't worry, I got it."

The phone kept on with its incessant ringing.

"Avery, just wait a damn second. Don't—"

I ducked past him, head down. "I'm going to head out." With a wave of my hand, I gestured at his phone. "Have fun with that."

Vibrant cursing was all I heard as I hustled away, getting lost in the crowds of the French Quarter.

This was for the best. Kissing Asher—kissing a *cop*— would be a disaster of epic proportions. Like the city's politicians, half of the police force in New Orleans were as crooked as they came.

New Orleans has been corrupt since 1718, Jay used to joke while we sat at the dinner table. *It's all this city knows.*

My mother would laugh, a gentle sound that always soothed me.

My stepfather would smirk.

And now, as I wound my way through throngs of people on Bourbon, my blood ran cold.

I could want Asher until the end of my days, but unless I could determine that his connections with Tabitha and the two dead men were nothing more than a coincidence, it was best that I kept far, far away from the brooding sergeant.

Something told me that that would be easier said than done.

And when I snicked my lock closed after entering the Sultan's Palace ten minutes later, I peered out the peephole, just in case I wasn't truly alone.

9

LINCOLN

"Take a seat, Sergeant."

What remained of my erection died at the sight of my lieutenant's *I-eat-small-children-for-breakfast* expression when I knocked on his office door. Stefan Delery had always been a ruthless motherfucker—I'd halfway convinced myself over the years that he'd been born with a stick shoved up his ass, and everyone in the district knew better than to piss the man off.

Everyone except for me.

I lowered myself in the chair opposite his, keeping my feet evenly planted on the tiled floor as I settled in for what was indubitably going to be an ass-chewing. "I'm surprised to see you here this late at night, L-T." I kept my tone passive when I added, "It's got to be way past your bedtime."

Nothing in the man's face twitched, not even his mustache.

"How long have we known each other, Asher?"

His question came like an unexpected left hook to the face when you're prepared for a right fist. Refusing to show my surprise, I murmured, "Are we counting the first time we met, when we were so obliterated that we rode the streetcar Uptown and back to the Quarter four times before we realized we were on a fast track to nowhere?"

Delery stared at me, his green eyes unblinking.

Christ, this wasn't going to go well.

Scrubbing a palm over my mouth, I let out a pent-up breath. "You were my sergeant when I was first assigned out in the East. Ten years ago."

"First night you were there a car blew up."

Despite the years since, the memories of licking flames and torched steel teasing at my combat boots, as I rounded the explosion, still hadn't been erased.

Feeling as though I'd just swallowed the fumes from the roasting engine, I said, "You told me to find the perp."

"And you did." Lines fanned out from Delery's eyes, as much of a smile as he'd ever given since his wife had passed two years earlier. "You were that crazy fucker running into the flames with no gear on but your damn duty belt, not a worry about your safety."

The silver lining about having nothing to live for was that taking a risk wasn't terrifying. I had no one at home to return to, no kids to tuck into bed or a wife to press into my side as we fell asleep after a long day.

I'd been alone since birth, an unwanted child who'd been dropped in foster care at an early age.

I dropped my elbows to my knees. "Where are you going with this, Stefan?" We'd known each other for years, had worked side-by-side through some of the roughest cases of the last decade in this city. "I know you didn't ask me to come in here past midnight so we could shoot the shit about the good old days."

"You've always been a good cop because you're fearless, Ash. You're levelheaded. That's the *exact* reason I put in a request to have you transferred here when you passed the sergeant's test three years ago." Delery leaned in, forearm on the desk, his closed-off expression unraveling into twitching mustaches, grinding teeth, and narrowed eyes. "I wanted that calm motherfucker who ran into the flames and then didn't lose his goddamn *shit* when he caught the perp."

Pressure built in my chest.

I needed to stay calm. Hell, I needed fresh air. The office suddenly felt stifling, even though I'd been in here dozens of times over the last three years since my transfer from New Orleans East to the French Quarter.

Hands balling into fists on my thighs, I kept the top half of my body, waist-up, completely nonchalant. I wouldn't react. I wouldn't lose my cool. I wouldn't—

Delery did none of the above.

"You chose the wrong asshole to throw a fist at tonight," he snapped, voice rising with furor. "The wrong fucking asshole." With one hand, he shoved at a stack of manila folders off the desk, sending them soaring to the floor.

The papers scattered like confetti.

"Did you read my report? Those *kids* publicly assaulted two females tonight. I got physical. It happens, and I wrote it up as a use-of-force." It was damn hard not to yell or demand understanding, but that wouldn't help me. Not when Delery was out for blood. *My* blood, that much was clear. "Maybe I should have stepped aside. Let two innocent girls become victims just because I hadn't stayed in my place."

"You chose the son of Pershing University's president for your little showdown."

Just like that, every argument died on my tongue.

Every. Last. One.

"Marcus Hampton called his daddy as soon as the guys

on the platoon brought him and his buddies to lockup, and no one—and I do mean *no one*—stood a chance once Joshua Hampton got involved."

I knew "Big" Hampton from assignments I'd worked at Pershing's football stadium as a rookie. Tall guy, a real bastard. He had his toes dipped in all of New Orleans' muddy waters, particularly those that made his coffers heavier and the women on his arm more attractive. In the years since he'd taken office, no one dared challenge the president of Pershing University.

And he'd never liked me much, not after his second wife had flirted with the "hot cop" right in front of him.

Sometimes New Orleans was really just too small.

I met Delery's gaze. "Big Hampton know it was me?"

All I was given in response was a slow nod that might as well have said *you're screwed.*

Raking my fingers through my hair, I slouched down in the chair and brought my fingers up to undo the top button of my Class B's. "What a fuckin' night." Which was, of course, the understatement of the century.

Delery matched my posture and did me one even better: he unpinned his badge from his chest and dropped it on the desk. My gaze latched onto the gold as it spun in a half-circle before falling flat on its back.

Symbolism if I'd ever seen one.

"He's already had words with Harlonne." At Delery's mention of our police chief, I barely held back a cringe. "Big Hampton wants you out of the force, Asher. No one touches his son, least of all a dirty cop. His words, not mine."

I was a dirtier cop than most, but no one knew that.

No one but Joshua Hampton, who now wanted my head on a platter.

It was assuredly *not* a great day to be me.

"So that's that, then?" I laughed, and even to my own ears, it sounded bitter. Angry. I had every right to be. I'd invested *years* into the NOPD, into the politics of New Orleans, into—

I cut those thoughts short, clenching my fists on my knees and tipping my head back to stare at the popcorn-raised ceiling. If it weren't Hampton holding the reins, there wouldn't be an issue. But there were three men you didn't cross in this city:

Joshua "Big" Hampton.

Jay Foley.

Jason Ambideaux.

I had the luxury of being on the shit list of two of the three "J's" that ran ship here.

"I talked with Harlonne an hour ago," Delery said, his voice low as though he worried someone might overhear him, "and we're not going to get rid of your sorry ass."

Relief sank into my limbs. "Thanks, L-T. Christ, it's been a hell of a—"

The lieutenant's mustache twitched as he averted his gaze. "Unfortunately, we've got to keep up appearances. Which means that we're cutting you a D-1. You're suspended, effective now."

Suspended? Back snapping straight, I dropped a fist to the desk and leaned in. "For how long? A week? Two weeks?"

Green eyes swiveled to meet mine. "For as long as it takes for Big Hampton to calm the hell down, *Sergeant*. We don't want to lose you—you're too damn good—and the men here respect you. But there's some shit we just can't get around and there's some people we don't need breathing down our necks, you hear me?" Like a mirror image, Delery brought a balled hand down on the desk. "Hampton is one of those people, as we both know. So, you're going to sit your ass out until shit gets quiet again, and when it looks like you aren't about to be ripped a new asshole because you touched the man's kid, we'll welcome you back with open arms and a bouquet of flowers."

"Can we skip the flowers and go straight for the beer, at least?"

Delery's eyes crinkled again. "That'll have to be approved by Harlonne." Once again, his face turned somber when he rapped his knuckles on the desk. "Give me your badge and your gun, Ash. Let's get this over with."

Fifteen minutes later, my feet hit the concrete steps outside of the district station, and I might as well have been stripped naked.

No badge.

No police ID.

No department-issued .40 on my hip.

For the next however long, I wasn't Sergeant Lincoln Asher.

Just Lincoln Asher, and nothing about my suspension was a good thing.

No, I was just fucked.

10

AVERY

"You need a life."

My fingers froze on the computer keyboard at the sound of Katie's voice. Minimizing the internet tab so that Katie couldn't scope out anything over my shoulder, I twisted on the couch to face her. "I have a life."

"Let me amend that," she said, coming around the edge of the couch to take the opposite side. She sprawled out, legs tangled on the middle cushions, and nabbed a pillow to hold to her chest. "Ahem. You need to get *laid*."

Like she'd pulled him out of thin air, my mind immediately brought forth a visual of Lincoln Asher. Warming at just the thought of him, I closed the laptop and set it on the coffee table. When Katie wanted to have a discussion, there was no stopping her. It seemed futile to pretend otherwise.

And, honestly, maybe I did need to talk to her—to *someone*—about what I felt for Asher. Which was lust, nothing more, nothing less. Just plain and simple lust.

As though sensing my indecision, Katie grinned. "My boys are willing to take care of you."

If I'd been drinking something, I would have come up

spluttering. As it was, I choked on thin air and gave myself a little shake. "I'm not—" More coughing. *Wonderful.* Nothing said "virgin" more than being unable to even have a conversation about sex. Clearing my throat, I tried again. "That's great, but I'm, uh, not having sex with George and Tyler."

Katie snagged her lower lip with her teeth. "What about George and Matt?"

I blinked. "What happened to Tyler?" Swinging my gaze to Katie's bedroom, I tacked on, "Tyler was balls' deep a week ago."

"Yeahhh, about that." My roommate shrugged, then flicked away imaginary lint from her shoulder. "Turns out that he didn't really like being *balls' deep* when another guy was dick deep, if you know what I mean."

Really, I shouldn't laugh. I *shouldn't* but the laughter bubbled up anyway. "You're kidding, right? Tyler bailed because you wanted him to participate instead of just jerking off in the corner like a voyeur?"

"I guess being that close to another dick made him feel uncomfortable."

I stared at her, hard. "You met him at a gay club, Katie, while he was back on leave. The man was oiled up and grinding on dicks when you waltzed in there."

"Okay! Fine, fine." She rolled her eyes, pillow going over her face. "Turns out that he wanted *me* to watch them together and let's be honest . . . I can be self-centered when it comes to sex. I wanted to be the center of attention and watching them fuck each other wasn't my idea of a good time."

"And the truth comes out!" I saluted her, one finger to my temple. "So, Tyler's off the table."

"Well, he's off the table for *me*." The pillow flung to the side as she sat up, a grimace pulling at her features. "But that doesn't mean he's off the table for you, so long as you've got another guy there with you. One word and Tyler will be hard and waiting."

But would he be as hard as Asher?

I blushed at the thought, then cursed myself for blushing in the first place. I'd felt the hard imprint of his erection against my belly, so what? It didn't mean anything. Plus, there was the whole I-shouldn't-be-looking-at-a-cop factor to consider.

One wrong move and he could out me completely, and then where would I be?

Possibly dead.

Probably dead.

Involuntarily, my gaze flicked to the closed laptop on the table again—a refurbished one that didn't have all the latest bells and whistles but certainly did the trick. I had no reason to suspect that Asher was the person who'd killed Josef Banterelli and Micah Welsh, but after following paper trails all night . . . Well, I wouldn't be surprised if he knew who'd been behind their ill-timed deaths.

And that was something I needed to discover quickly because if that list had any commonalities, then I needed to ensure Tabby was far, far away from here before her turn came around.

Maybe seeing Asher wouldn't be such a bad idea . . .

"You've got that face again."

Careful not to show my ace, I offered an easy grin. "*That* face? Last I was aware, I only had one of them."

From the way Katie studied me, it was clear she didn't believe me.

"Don't even play that game," she said, tossing back her hair and snuggling deeper into the couch cushions, pillow once again clamped to her chest. "I've known you long enough to know when you're up to something, Ave. Hell, I might be the *only* person who knows you well enough to figure out when you're up to no good."

I shifted on the couch, uncomfortable under her acute assessment. "I promise that I'm up to only good." Flashing her a wink, I prayed that she'd let the matter drop. Talking about sex I could handle, but whenever Katie hooked her claws into me, demanding that I open up and spill my heart out, it generally meant for a few awkward days after.

It wasn't that I didn't trust her.

Of every person I'd met since my mother's death, Katie was perhaps the *only* person I trusted.

But even that trust went only so far.

All it would take is one slip-up from her at the club to the wrong patron and I'd be on the run. *Again.* I'd spent years looking over my shoulder, terrified that if I made the wrong move, I'd find myself at my stepfather's mercy. And, this time, there wouldn't be a merciful, faceless man to let me escape into the night.

Katie stared at me, then announced, "I need wine." Jumping up from the couch, she headed for our kitchenette. "You want wine?"

I wanted to research the two murders and hopefully connect the dots to Tabby. Still, Katie wasn't just my roommate, she was my best friend. I wouldn't take it for granted, now or ever.

Folding my legs beneath me, I propped an arm on the back of the couch. "Do we have any chardonnay left?"

Katie pulled open the fridge and a wine bottle emerged two seconds later. "We're skipping glasses tonight." Bottle in hand, she twisted off the top and tossed it on the kitchen counter before moving back to the couch, where she collapsed with absolutely no grace. "To girls' night," she said, lifting the bottle high.

"To girls' night," I echoed, gripping the chardonnay bottle by the neck when she passed it over after taking a pull from its mouth. The chilled wine slipped down my throat, and I tried to ignore Katie's unwavering stare. I passed the bottle back over to her. "So, everything going okay at work late—"

"I went through your files."

My heart flexed. Nerves. Fear. And, yes, beneath all the panic, anger.

I pressed my trembling hands to my lap and did my best to control that same tremble in my voice when I spoke. "Those files don't belong to you." I didn't succeed. My voice quivered, as did my entire body. "That wasn't . . . they aren't . . . you can't just go through people's belongings because you feel like it, Katie. T-that's *bullshit*."

She chugged the wine like a professional, then clasped the bottle between her knees. "It's not bullshit, *Avery*."

Every limb, muscle, tendon, went rigid at the way she uttered my name. There was nothing in the filing cabinet that could discriminate me—or that mentioned Laurel Peyton anywhere—but, still, worry cramped in my belly. *What if she knew?* I didn't even have the opportunity to open my mouth before she plowed on, all accusing fingers and narrowed eyes.

"It's not *bullshit*. We've been living together for years and I know close to nothing about you. *Nothing*. You've never had sex. You didn't drink liquor until you were twenty-one like some good girl from God-knows-where. You're twenty-five. *That's* what I know."

Desperation clawed at me, a silent urging for me to pack my things and get the hell out of dodge. Where I would go, I had no idea. Maybe it was time that I had no destination. That I left New Orleans.

And years of careful research would be washed down the drain, not to mention that if I left, there was a good chance Tabby could end up just like Josef and Micah. I couldn't even stomach the possibility.

Not that I had any idea of how to worm my way out of this showdown with my roommate.

A deep breath did nothing to calm my jitters. "Listen, Katie, I—"

"I'm over the lying," Katie marched on. "Do you realize just how much you owe me? I mean, yeah, you pay your own way and never ask for even a dime. But this rental property? It's in my name. Same with all of our utilities. I like you, Avery. I'm a girl who operates on gut instinct, and I've always liked you. But I can't—" She shoved her fingers through her hair. Drew in an uneven, shuddering breath. "I could kick you out right now. I could tell you to pack your bags and you'd be shit out of luck within the court of law."

It was definitely time for wine.

I reached forward, fingers ready to grasp the bottle, when it was snatched up and away.

My fingers caught nothing but air.

"You scared me last week, Ave, with those guys attacking you." Katie shook her head, and it was then that I saw the misery in her green eyes. She looked . . . well, she looked horrible. Exhausted.

"Kat—"

Another shake of her head, this one sharper than the last. "No, I need to . . . I need to get this out. You know that I don't have anyone. My parents are divorced; they remarried with so many more kids that I doubt they remember who I even am. I moved to New Orleans with some idiotic idea

that I'd find myself, and that, you know . . . my uncle might
want to take pity on his brother's wayward daughter." Her
lips curled in a bitter smile. "I found a stripper pole instead,
so we all know how *that* worked out. I tarnished the family
name, through and through. *Anyway,* what I'm trying to say
is, just like I'm all you've got, you're all *I've* got. And right
now, something could happen to you and you don't even
have a real ID."

A startled laugh leapt to my lips. "That's what this all
boils down to? Me having a fake ID?"

Katie tossed her pillow at my face, and I swatted it out of
the way before it made contact. "You know what I mean,"
she muttered, "you're like this . . . this *shadow* or something. I
don't know."

Strangely enough, that's how I felt. Like this city had
kept my secrets, and I'd been sheltered ever since.

Until now.

I couldn't reveal everything to Katie, no matter how
much I wanted to unload my burdens. There was still so
much I didn't understand . . . so much that eluded me. So
much that she simply couldn't know.

I dug my elbows into my knees, back hunched. *Say something.* It was either that or lose her completely, and the latter
wasn't an option. "I've lived in N'Orleans my entire life."
Ugh, not a great opener but it'd have to do. Lips parting, I
tried to find the words that would unruffle Katie's feathers
while still protecting my own. My gaze went to the laptop
again, and this time I didn't look away.

"Someone murdered my mother," I finally said, only to
hear Katie's shocked gasp. I didn't stop, in fear that her
sympathies would derail me. "I was young and I don't
remember much." The lie came out easily, even if I could
still hear the *boom!* of the pistol now as it fired. My shoulders

curled more, so much so that I nearly hugged my legs. Just as I had that night when I'd buried my face into my bent knees. Nausea gripped my insides, and I forced myself to continue. "I ran, back then."

From between her fingers, my roommate whispered, "You saw her die?"

The blood, yes. Her body, no. "I heard it." *Continued to hear it.* "I was a scared little girl who was even more frightened by who could hurt me. What I'm trying to say is, the fake ID and all that . . . the underworld of New Orleans doesn't stop at the clubs on Bourbon. You know that. Runners like me, there are hundreds of us. Thousands, maybe. I swear to you, I'm exactly where I need to be."

"But you don't want to . . ." Biting down on the pad of her thumb, her gaze jumped from my face to the wine bottle to the stray couch cushions. "You really don't mind the anonymity? The constant hiding? What if . . . what if you ever want to get married? You'll never tell your spouse that you're actually someone else?"

It didn't seem worth the trouble to tell her that marriage wasn't in the cards for me.

Marrying someone meant trusting them to put you first, and I was highly skeptical of *anyone* putting me first—especially a man. Lightly, I ran my fingers over my sweatpants, over my inner left knee, tracing the spot where words were inked into my skin as a reminder: *I bow to no man.*

A lesson Jay Foley ensured I would never forget.

When I smiled, it seemed to creak across my face. "I figure I'll cross that bridge when I get to it."

As though I'd passed some sort of test, she handed me the wine.

I'd told her close to nothing, and even that felt like an information overload.

Katie was bright colors and loud music.

I was darkness and silence.

She'd figure it out one day, and I could only swear to myself now that when shit finally hit the fan with Jay Foley after all these years, my best friend would be nowhere to be found. She'd be safe. And far, far away.

"Love you, Ave," she whispered, reaching out to squeeze my arm. "I'm sorry I went through your things."

"Don't worry about it." I returned the squeeze. "And love you too."

I thought of the files and notebooks I'd stashed in our unused cupboard above the refrigerator, files that included every ounce of information I'd accumulated over the years about my stepfather, along with any mention of my mother's death and my faked one in the newspapers.

Self-disgust clung to me.

I was good at hiding. Even better at deception.

And Katie would never know that the documents she'd found were nothing but decoys.

I brought the wine bottle to my mouth and took a large sip. I didn't deserve a friend like Katie, but that wasn't something I didn't already know.

You couldn't deserve a relationship when it was founded on a lie, and Katie, my roommate, my friend, my step-cousin, would never forgive me if she learned the truth.

Of that I had no doubt.

.

Growing up, I'd been the kid who skipped school and then skipped detention right after that on principle alone. No doubt about it, I'd been a little shit.

But there'd been one day in the ninth grade where I'd managed to keep my ass in class long enough to learn something. English literature. Ms. Mackenzie. She'd been the real reason I'd stuck around, and it was her that I had to thank for discovering *Dante's Inferno* and his nine circles of hell.

No one else had found the book intriguing, but to me, it'd felt like I'd found a bible of sorts. Or, at least, a bible for the permanently fallen.

Ms. Mackenzie had thought it funny to test us all, just a little pop quiz to determine in which circle of hell we'd find ourselves. A personality quiz of epic proportions.

The girls giggled into their palms.

The other guys sat forward because, yeah, death and destruction was their thing after playing endless rounds of video games after school.

And me . . . I'd worked down the eraser of my pencil to the nub as I filled out the multiple-choice options. Determined to evaluate my fate by a scaling system some dude had created centuries before I was even conceived.

Pencils down, Ms. Mackenzie asked that we stand when our "circle" was called upon after she read out the answers. The overall average determined which circle we would have found ourselves in had we existed in the book.

One by one, she read out the questions and which answers correlated with which circle.

One by one, everyone stood.

And, one by one, I'd noted that my peers rose in clusters, with most falling into Lust or Limbo, that halfway, in-between spot where you descended no lower but weren't allowed to enter Paradise.

Not me.

Question after question, I climbed to my feet to find myself in a new circle of hell.

Lust.

Greed.

Treachery.

Violence.

Anger.

Ms. Mackenzie paused, pencil eraser against her cheek, to stare at me when it was all said and done. "Looks like you're well-traveled, Lincoln," she said with wide, pretty blue eyes.

The me at fourteen years old had nothing on me at thirty-four, twenty years later, and as I entered my house a week after my implemented suspension, there was no denying that I was on the verge of revisiting every damn one of Dante's circles all over again.

The bastard sitting at my kitchen table, drinking my Scotch straight from the bottle, would have it no other way.

I snapped the door shut behind me and flicked the dead

bolt into place, not that it had done me any good tonight. Dropping my mail onto the entryway table, I schooled my features into the blank mask that had served me well for years.

Almost as well as the .19 tucked into the waistband of my jeans and the second one attached to the concealed ankle holster on my right leg. I'd been safer as a cop than I was now as a civilian, and the irony of that wasn't lost on me as I took an empty seat at the kitchen table, my back to the refrigerator.

Damn bastard had already taken the seat that kept his back to the wall, and I scraped my chair across the tile so that I had a clearer view of every possible entry into the kitchen.

"Don't trust me, Lincoln?"

I bristled at that sly, familiar tone. "Last time we were in the same room, you aimed your nine-millimeter at my thigh and fired. Twice."

Jason Ambideaux, New Orleans's most infamous real estate mogul, chuckled into my bottle of Scotch. "Ever hear of the saying, 'let bygones be bygones?'"

It took every last ounce of self-control I possessed not to pull out my gun and unload a clip into the man's head. *Breathe*, I warned myself, fingers digging into my thighs. "Should I remind you that you left me to bleed out?" *And that maybe I'd like to return the favor, finally.*

With his slicked-back hair, dyed black to hide the grays, and the sharp business suit he wore like a second skin, Ambideaux was the physical embodiment of the power he'd wielded over New Orleans for the last twenty years. He was the bane of every competitor's existence, and those who didn't acquiesce gallantly to his established rein eventually found themselves face-down in the swamps of the Atchafalaya Basin two hours outside of New Orleans.

My sixteenth birthday had been commemorated with my first Basin run, at Ambideaux's command.

On the way back to New Orleans, I'd pulled over on the I-10 and vomited until there was nothing left but me dry-heaving on the side of the highway as the clock struck midnight like some fucked up fairy tale. If Cinderella had been given a gun instead of some glass slippers, she wouldn't have lasted an hour in my life.

At Ambideaux's silence to my question, I filled it in for him, my temper close to snapping. "Nothing to say?" More silence, each passing second more grating on my nerves than the last.

And then, finally, the bastard spoke: "The scars are worse than they told me."

It was the wrong thing to say.

The Scotch bottle shattering on the tile coincided with the mouth of my .19 connecting with Ambideaux's forehead. The force drove his skull into the wall with a sickening thud, and it was there, in the deepest recesses of my soul, that whispered for me to pull the trigger.

Revenge delivered swiftly was never as satisfying, but, goddammit, it would feel *good*.

"You don't have the balls, son," Ambideaux said, voice as even as if he'd been discussing a play by play of the weather and not staring down the barrel of a pistol, "put down the gun."

I put the gun down all right—dragging it down the center of his face, over the slope of his straight, aristocratic nose, until it settled against the pulse beating at his neck like some sort of hickey of death. Only when Ambideaux's right eyebrow twitched tellingly did I growl, "It wasn't enough for you to just let me die, was it?" The mouth of the .19 dug in a little more, my finger resting on the trigger guard. "Nah, you had me driven out to the Atchafalaya and tossed in as fuckin' gator meat like the rest of them."

I met his dark eyes. Felt the way he struggled to swallow with my gun jammed against his throat. The grin that spread across my face was one born of vengeance. "What was it you told me right before you pulled the trigger? Oh, yeah." I leaned in, breath coasting across his face, finger lifting off the trigger guard. "I won't think any less of you when you piss your—"

Arms clamped around my throat, squeezing off my oxygen supply, dragging me backward.

Pft! Pft!

Splintering glass echoed in my ears as my gun went off before being torn from my hands. Vision swirling, I gasped for breath and let instinct take over, driving an elbow into the body behind me. My attacker was big, but I was bigger, and I dug in my heels and wrapped my hands around his forearms, fully prepared to flip the asshole right over my shoulder and put the .19 at my ankle to good use.

There was always a benefit to being a walking artillery.

With my full weight, I arched my back to get momentum and then snapped my body forward like a slingshot, thighs clenching, knees tight, core flexing. I felt my attacker's feet come off the floor behind me as I assumed his full weight, and I buckled down, tightening my muscles, ready to—

Cold metal to my forehead stilled the fight in me, and I glanced up, past the barrel of my own weapon, to Ambideaux. His slicked-back hair was disheveled, his pristine suit rumpled, his expression ambivalent.

"You done?"

A sneer caught in my throat, even as gravity dropped the

bastard on my back, back onto my kitchen floor. Not even a second passed before he'd readjusted his grip, massive arms binding me once again.

Ambideaux twisted away, setting the Glock on the table, out of my reach. "Sit his ass down and make sure he can't move."

Ambideaux's lackey shoved me into the chair I'd just vacated, then snapped handcuffs around my wrists, the *click-click-click* of metal sliding into place a completely unmistakable sound. "Benefits to breaking and entering a cop's house," he grunted brusquely, "you made this way too easy for me." He drew up another chair and positioned it behind me. A half-second later, familiar cold metal touched the back of my skull. "We're all set, boss."

My fingers flexed in the restraints.

Ambideaux planted his ass on the edge of the table, arms crossed over his chest. "You're still a hothead, Lincoln." He shook his head with a low laugh, like I hadn't just been seconds away from ending his life. "Once a hothead, always a hothead. Damn, but I wish I'd been there when you punched Little Hampton. Would have made my year."

Grinning at my expense, he added, "Actually, you would have made my life a hell of a lot easier if you'd just"—he mimicked slicing his throat open—"finished off the deed."

When I opened my mouth to speak, the pressure point at the back of my skull increased. Narrowing my eyes, I gave that pressure right back, leaning my weight into that gun, challenging the owner to get on with it and shoot me.

After a moment, the pressure slackened, and my chest hitched with minute relief.

"I'm going to assume you didn't bust in here to reminisce about the good old times *or* talk about how much you want Hampton's kid dead." I eyed the gun on the table, then redirected my attention back to my old boss. "So why don't we cut to the chase and get this over with? Fill in the blank for me. You're here because of . . ."

"Impatient still, too." Ambideaux's mouth quirked up in a humorless grin. "It's like the last twelve years haven't existed, wouldn't you say?"

I bit the inside of my cheek to keep from mouthing off. I wasn't a hothead, not in the way he remembered. "Just answer the question, Jason. You're here . . . *why*?"

"I heard about your suspension."

Just like that, my heart threatened to leap out of my chest. I yanked forward, caught back by the handcuffs, and then grit my teeth. "It's not happening."

Ambideaux sank to his haunches before me, and then the gun at my head angled forward, leaving me no choice but to dip my chin and keep my eyes on the real estate mogul. If he were closer, I'd drive my foot into his chest hard enough to send him sailing backward.

But Jason Ambideaux hadn't spent years working toward being one of the three most feared men in New Orleans without learning a thing or two. He squatted just out of reach, one hand on his knee, the other on his inner thigh as he watched me.

"A deal is a deal, son," he murmured, looking not even a little remorseful about playing puppeteer with my life. My mother's life. "We agreed that for however long you were on the job, I'd leave you alone, but you've never been good at stepping back from playing hero." His dark eyes roved over my face. "Tell me, did you feel like a champ to know that you saved that poor girl from being raped? Or perhaps the other one, too . . . the one a colleague of mine spotted you with outside of the station last week?"

My vision flashed red, my chest heaving with labored breathing as the implication behind his words hit me.

He grinned wolfishly. "Ah, you're just figuring it out. Good, that's good." He tapped his knee as though debating on giving up information. "In case you're still concerned, Casey's doing quite well. I believe she opted for a gift card in exchange for her troubles, but I had something more sentimental in mind."

Sentimental, my ass. Visions of the poor girl sinking into the Atchafalaya Basin etched across my retina, and it was like I was sixteen all over again, feeling the urge to retch after tossing my first dead body into the swampy marshlands. My scars prickled with memories better left forgotten, and I swallowed the bile rising in my throat.

"You've always been such a saint, Lincoln," Ambideaux said in a contemptuous tone, "but you can't save them all."

Between clenched teeth, I ground out, "I won't help you. Put a bullet in the back of my head if it'll make you feel better, I don't give a shit."

"And leave your mother as she is? No, I don't think so." Knees popping as he stood, Ambideaux picked up the Glock and stared at it, his gaze almost wistful. "A deal is a deal, Sergeant, and you've already paid in blood. I agreed to leave you be for as long as you remained with the NOPD, but it seems that you've recently been suspended."

There was no end to the hatred that thrived in my veins. It pulsed, and, like poison, spread through me like an infection. "You fucking bastard," I spat, "you organized all of this. You really think you can—"

The pistol came out of nowhere, but holy hell, I felt it.

My head whipped to the side as the barrel made contact with my scarred cheek. The metallic taste of blood spurted in my mouth, pain erupting in my tongue as the impact forced me to bite down.

And all the while, the gun at my skull never wavered. If anything, the pressure increased, forcing me to look down completely, chin to my chest.

Like I was bowing to Ambideaux, no matter the fact that I was still slouched on the chair, hands handcuffed behind my back.

The longer I sat there, the drowsier I became. It wasn't my first concussion and I knew the symptoms well.

Stay awake. You need to stay awake.

It'd be easy to surrender to the darkness, to slip into the abyss and ride out the numbness of my existence until everything went black. Permanently.

Ambideaux had other plans.

His fingers sank into my hair, pulling my head up. I blinked and then blinked again, but no matter how many times my lids fell shut and opened again, he remained a hazy mirage that wouldn't sharpen.

"This is how it's going to work, son," he said, voice chipper for the first time since I'd walked in to find him drinking my Scotch. "I've got a little list that I need you to take care of for me. Knowing you, you'll get it squared away for me before you're back to work. And if you're not"—his fingers tightened their grip on my hair and I swallowed a hiss—"I'll just make sure your suspension ends up being just a little longer. How's that sound?"

He let me go and set the Glock on the table again, only to ferret around in his suit jacket. He revealed a spiral-bound notebook that he tossed at my feet. "Two are already done, which means that all that's left are three Basin runs . . . once you've taken care of business, of course."

My gaze latched onto the compact notebook, my stomach turning at the sight of the familiar names. Two dead—Josef Banterelli and Micah Welsh. I hadn't seen them in years, but I'd still felt a pang of remorse over old times' sake when I'd heard about their deaths on the news. It was on the tip of my tongue to ask why Ambideaux had chosen the Mississippi River as their final resting ground, but the momentary concern was swept away under the frustration bubbling under my skin.

Twelve years. I'd spent *twelve* years putting this shit with Ambideaux behind me, and even if I'd done runs recently for a few people, *nothing* had ever been as bad as what Jason enjoyed tasking his "employees" with.

"I should point out that if you're hoping to get out of this, I've left an identical one of those notepads in your desk at the station." Grinning widely, Ambideaux straightened his suit and turned for the door. "And as we all know, *Sergeant*, you aren't allowed to set foot on NOPD property for the length of your suspension or risk being permanently terminated. What a predicament you've found yourself in, wouldn't you say? At the risk of working for *me* permanently, I suggest you take care of what I've given you. Your mother will thank you, I'm sure."

The door swung open and Ambideaux strolled out, whistling like a damn lunatic.

Another ten minutes passed before the bastard at my back stepped away and flashed me a gold key that he set on the table—on the *other* side of the table—before following his boss out.

Leaving me alone to my past that was, once again, my present and my foreseeable future.

The sinner.

The executioner.

The man who belonged in every circle of hell.

12

AVERY

He was here.

Surprise snapped my back straight, twining up my legs as my feet ground to a halt by the bar, sending my cocktail up, up, up, until the straw fit between my teeth and I'd guzzled half a Hurricane.

"You going to slow down there, girl?" Katie asked from behind the bar. Unlike mine, my roommate's shirt was tugged down low to show off the goods to the patrons, and with every shake of the cocktail mixer, her breasts shook almost as much for the crowd.

Meanwhile, I looked like a nun in comparison—jeans paired with ankle-high boots, topped off with an oversized sweater that did nothing for my figure. All that I was missing was the chastity belt and we could call it a day. My lack of sex appeal had never bothered me, and it hadn't bothered me as I'd waltzed out of the Sultan's Palace and walked the three blocks to the club with Katie.

Now it bothered me.

Because of *him*, I wanted to tie my sweater up around my ribcage and prove that I could be just as enticing as the

women gyrating on the bar tops. Him—Lincoln Asher. New
Orleans police sergeant. Arrogant asshole. Almost-kisser of
women up against brick buildings when they weren't
expecting it and were hardly prepared to get in on the whole
kiss him back bit.

To say nothing of his ill-timed phone call.

My cheeks flamed at the memory, and even though it'd
been only a little over a week since then, I could still feel the
grain of the brick scraping against the backs of my arms, as
well as the constant, on-loop realization that Asher had
smelled acutely like aftershave and hot male.

I finished the Hurricane and set it on the bar. "I'm good,"
I told Katie, ignoring the way she eyed me skeptically with a
once-over.

She'd wanted me to come tonight and live a little. *You
need to pick up a guy, Avery*, she'd said, fluffing her hair in the
mirror as we got ready. *An orgasm will un-crankify you.*

I hadn't come tonight with the plan to find myself an
orgasm, but I hadn't expected to find Asher here either. And
if there was ever a man who looked like he whipped up
orgasms for a living, it was him.

It was now or never. I'd managed twenty-five years
without feeling an attraction for a man, and if I didn't hop
on the opportunity now, there was a good chance I'd go
another twenty-five years without feeling this all-consuming
need again.

You never cared about orgasms before you met him.

I thrust the thought away, burying it deep, as I waved off
Katie's concern. "I'm good! All good. You go do your thing."

Tossing a garnish into a margarita, she shoved it at a
patron and took his card. "You sure?" she asked me, turning
for the cash register along the back of the bar. "You hardly
ever drink. Hold on, let me get you some water."

"Katie."

Over the din of the crowd and the DJ playing a song from the latest Top 100, she cut me a look and then gave a self-deprecating roll of her eyes. "Okay, yeah, I'm mama-bearing right now. I'll chill."

Wanting to perk her up, I said, "I can't find myself an orgasm in this crowd if you're hovering."

The guy to my left winked at me and then grabbed his junk. "I know where you can find one."

I smiled sweetly. "I'd rather eat nails."

Face contorting with displeasure, he snatched his drink off the bar and disappeared into the crowd, only for Katie to place a plastic cup of water in front of me a second later. "Guess he wasn't the one?" she asked, right brow arched high.

Not even a little.

"I've got someone else in mind."

Her left brow rose to meet the right, but a guy hollering at the other end of the bar cut her response short. With a *behave-yourself* finger wave in my direction, she grabbed a rag off the counter and slung it over one shoulder before hightailing it down to the customer.

I waited, giving her a moment to get lost in the frenzy of a weekend night in the French Quarter, and then I craned my neck, seeking another glimpse of the man determined to drive me insane.

The only man I could envision between my legs.

Fingers grazed my left hand, shockingly warm in comparison to the ice-cold cocktail I'd just sipped, and I pulled away from the unfamiliar touch.

I didn't get far.

A strong hand wrapped around my wrist, stalling my flight, and then it was *his* voice that I heard next to my ear, rustling the strands of my hair, enflaming me as though my body operated on his command.

"Goin' somewhere?"

It was the same question he'd asked when we'd first met in Jackson Square. The same gravel-pitched voice. This time, unlike the last, I was in no mood to run away.

I wanted what he'd offered me in a dark alley against the police precinct a week ago. I wanted what I hadn't been bold enough to take then—pleasure, sex, the mutual understanding that it was a one-time deal only.

Simple. Uncomplicated.

Perfect.

And, yes, maybe curiosity still lingered as to why he'd had that notebook in his desk drawer. The one with Tabby's name on it . . . along with the names of two dead men. Getting up, close, and personal with Asher killed two birds with one stone.

Though right now the only bird I wanted to know more about was why, of all people, *he* was the one to flip my proverbial switch.

He stood so close that my shoulder grazed his chest when I turned toward him. My gaze lifted from his black, ribbed sweater, past the thick column of his throat to his rugged face. Under the bar's florescent lighting, the jagged scars across his cheek might as well have been a calling card for DANGER AHEAD.

My entire life had been spent sequestered in the shadows, and I didn't know what it said about me that I was willing to step into that danger now, to hell with the consequences.

"Following me again?" I asked boldly.

"I was already here."

He said it casually, with absolute conviction, and I was

suddenly thankful for the shadows, which hid my flush. Flirting wasn't my forte, and it figured that I couldn't even manage a decent conversation starter with him.

Of course, he'd been here. I'd spotted him along the back corner, seated at a table with someone I didn't recognize, minutes after I'd entered the club and taken a seat at the bar. I should have turned around then. Walked out. Gone home.

Instead, I'd downed a Hurricane for fortitude and waited for Asher to notice me in return.

Now, his hand skimmed my forearm, my bicep, not stopping until his palm settled on my neck, his thumb brushing the sensitive skin of the underside of my jaw. Goosebumps flared to life on my arms as I buried a swallow, worried that he might sense my spiking nerves. A guy like him—if he caught even a scent of my inexperience—would move on to the next girl in seconds.

I forced myself to meet his gaze casually, like my body wasn't turning into liquid fire at the barest hint of his touch.

"You're nuzzling my hand like you're regretting us stoppin' the other night, Avery."

Shock filtered down my spine, jerking my shoulders at the truth. I *was* nuzzling his hand. Shamelessly, too. Briefly, my eyes squeezed shut. If I hadn't seen him tonight, if he hadn't appeared here as though my dreams had sketched his muscular build into reality, I wouldn't have sought him out.

It's officially *now or never*.

With feigned confidence and a rapidly beating heart, I pressed my palm to his abdomen. Even through the fabric of his sweater, it was impossible to ignore the hard ridges of his muscles and the way they flexed with every breath he pulled into his lungs. I counted those inhalations like they were my own, and nearly gave into the little devil on my shoulder, which whispered for me to push his shirt up and touch him, skin to skin.

As I all but petted him, his blue eyes never veered from my face. If I were weaker, I'd let the intensity of his stare get to my head—let myself think more of this moment than what the facts bluntly told me.

And the facts were simple: tonight was about lust only, nothing more.

I shifted my hand upward, needing to level out the playing field. "Your heart is beating fast, Sergeant," I murmured, loud enough to be heard over the crowd. "Don't tell me you're nervous."

Mouth firming into a thin line, his hand locked around my wrist again. "Don't twist this into something that it's not. I don't get nervous."

I lifted my brows. "Because you're such a stoic cop?"

"Because I don't do commitment."

"Perfect," I said with a small nod, "I'm not looking for that either." Jerking my chin toward the front door, which sat beyond a sea of grinding couples, I added, "Should we go?"

His grip tightened. "What changed your mind?"

He had changed my mind. With my back to the police station and his big hands on my body, something in me had cracked. Broken free. Like a drug, I was hooked on the feeling of liberation already, and Asher had only given me a small taste of what might come after submitting to the pleasure he wielded. Refusing to show him that he held the upper hand in our little dynamic, I shot back, "Why do your scars look like they've been busted back open?"

Lincoln Asher responded exactly as I expected him to—a careful mask that concealed every trace of emotion. No twisted lips, no narrowed eyes, no steam that billowed out of his nostrils like a cartoon caricature from my youth. No, Asher was stone silent, his rugged face appearing only more tormented with its new pinkish tint to the old, flattened scars.

Old intersecting with the new. If I thought he'd tell me what had gone down, I would have pushed harder.

As it was, he eliminated the remaining distance between us, forcing me to tilt my head back or cut eye contact and cede this round to him.

"If we leave, I'm going to fuck you," he murmured, all games tossed to the side. "Do you get that? There's no third chances. You either agree or you go find someone else to play this cat-and-mouse chase."

I was grateful that my hand was on *his* heart and not the other way around. Mine thundered in my chest with ridiculous fervor. "I'm not running away . . . Does that answer your question?"

In a million years, I never could have anticipated the way he lifted my hand and pressed his mouth to the soft skin of my inner wrist. Heat, scorched heat—it licked at my feet as Asher's blue gaze zeroed in on my face, his mouth hovering a hair's breadth over my wrist. "Your pulse is beating fast, Avery," he said, voice low, a wicked glint in his eyes, "don't tell me you're nervous."

A gasp lodged in my throat as he caught my fingers with his and turned to wind through the crowd, never severing our connection. Throngs of people pushed inward, forcing me to squeeze through or be left behind.

But Asher never released me.

His shoulders were wide, his back broad, his waist trim, and the only thought on repeat in my head was, *This is about to happen.*

Katie would be so proud, and I was . . . at odds even in my own head.

I wasn't ready, not fully prepared for stripping my control and handing over the reins, the power, to a man I hardly knew, but I couldn't say no. Couldn't walk away. He did this to me. Twisted all my emotions inside out and set me on fire with nothing but the rough way he uttered my name.

The air outside was humid, thick, and my hands immediately turned clammy.

I'm not nervous, I reminded myself as we cut to the right, around a group of people mingling outside, smoking cigarettes.

I've got this, I told myself as Asher tugged me down the next street, onto St. Phillip.

Act confident, I ordered myself as my back gently hit the wall of a building and all I saw was Asher.

"Hands on the brick," came his low command.

He's recreating the other night.

I sucked in as much air as my lungs would allow and then set my hands against the building. The brick scraped my palms and my fingers curled in, mimicking the way my toes did the same in my shoes.

Asher leaned into me, lending me his weight, eliminating any chance for my escape into the night. The scent of his aftershave tickled my nose, and I fought the urge to tuck my nose into the crook of his neck and smell him.

"What next?" I whispered, though I tried damn hard to sound unaffected.

Blue eyes met mine, startling me with the heat that I saw there. His face was uncompromising in its firm lines and scars, but his gaze . . . *oh God,* for the first time I wondered if a mistake was knocking on my door. He looked at me like I was the first meal he'd been given after years of starvation. It was carnal, the way his gaze devoured me. Needy. Raw. And when his chest brushed mine as he inhaled, every ounce of heat in those startling blue eyes of his made me feel like I'd been stumbling through life just to get to this moment with him.

This man was dangerous, wicked, and as though my brain had been usurped by someone else, I heard the words trip off my tongue: "Don't make me wait, Sergeant."

Like a candle being snuffed out, the intensity in his gaze wavered, flickering, before sparking back to life again with a ferociousness that had me inching back . . . but there was nowhere to go and nowhere to escape.

"Don't make threats you can't keep," he warned.

"How do you know I won't keep them?"

His hands landed on mine to drag them up until they were on either side of my head. Pinned.

"For tonight," he growled, "you belong to me. Do you understand?"

And then his mouth was on mine, and I could only summon one word, even if it existed only in my head: *yes.*

13

AVERY

A sher claimed my mouth as though he was starved for something only I could give him.

Blood surged in my head, clouding my vision, and I slammed my eyes shut against everything but the feel of him. The heat of his big body, the way his belt buckle was like a brand against my sweater-covered stomach. One masculine hand released mine to coast down my body, following the swell of my breasts to stop at the dip of my waist.

And all the while, he kissed me. It wasn't gentle and it wasn't soft and even though this was the first kiss I'd ever given a man willingly, I refused to ask Asher to slow down. To take it easy on me.

To—

A gasp broke free from my chest as he nudged my chin to the side, his lips coming to nip the skin just below my jawline. My hand, the one still locked by his to the wall, flexed forward, seeking the softness of his hair.

Asher readjusted his grip, hand splayed over my wrist. I might as well have been chained, I had no slack.

"Until I say otherwise," he rumbled against my neck, "you're going to have to take it." He soothed the bite with a swipe of his tongue, making my pulse skyrocket and my heels come off the cement as I strained closer. "Can you do that, Avery?"

All I saw were the backs of my eyelids when I half-gasped out, "Anyone ever tell you that you're a pompous asshole?"

Another nip from him, another gasp from me, and then a roughly uttered, "I'm a cop. Never had anyone call me a sweetheart before while on the job."

If I weren't so turned on, I would have laughed. As it was, I could hardly think straight. "Devil's more like it," I said, moving into complete shameless territory when I tilted my head a little more in a silently encouraged, *I-want-more-of-that.*

Asher, asshole that he was, either didn't recognize the request or decided to play dumb because his weight lifted from mine. "I prefer sinner, actually." He tangled our fingers together and, before I could even plan for what he'd had up his sleeve, he spun me around, chest to the wall. "But I'm willing to play whatever role you want me to tonight."

My chest heaved at my new position, the backs of my hands cushioning my cheek from the brick.

You're going to have to take it.

His words rang loud in my head, and there was no doubt about it: I was in trouble.

Because Asher's gruffness, the domineering way he put me where he wanted me, didn't make me want to run and never look back.

Not even a little.

Instead I arched my back, seeking his touch. I twisted my upper body, my left ear taking the place of my cheek on my hands as I looked for him over my shoulder. He was there, less than a foot away, and for a moment, I did nothing but study him.

In every other one of our interactions, he'd been dressed in his NOPD uniform. The dark slacks. The jacket over the crisp button-down shirt with the shiny, gold badge pinned to his breast pocket—so respectable. Honorable. An upstanding citizen of the first order.

Tonight, he looked like the devil I'd claimed him to be, and it was an intoxicating contradiction.

Dark jeans, the even darker sweater with the sleeves rolled up to his elbows.

But it wasn't the clothes that had my heart racing, nor even his powerful body.

No, it was the wild look in his blue gaze. With the shadows splicing across his face, his features were drawn tight, almost savage in the way he watched me. Drawing in a steadying breath, I licked my lips and wondered if the darkness in me had found its echo in him.

"Don't make me call you an asshole again for making me wait," I whispered, then mentally cursed myself for coming just short of begging him.

If he reacted with a smile to my hot retort, I couldn't make it out as I turned back to the wall.

I did, however, hear the clip of his heavy boot hit the cement. One step. Two steps. And then he was there behind me, hands coming to rest on the building, bracketing me within his embrace. "You going to let me take you right here?" he drawled softly. "Is that what you want?" With one hand, he gently swept my dark hair over one shoulder, and then—oh God—he fisted the strands and everything in me snapped with instant awareness.

Fight or flight.

Not me.

Letting instinct overrule all rational thought, I ground my ass backward, right into his crotch, just like every couple in the nightclub we'd left twenty minutes ago. I was rewarded for my boldness—his guttural groan echoed in my ear, his hand clamping down on my hip to still . . . no, no, he wasn't even stopping me. If anything, he crowded me further, eliminating whatever distance remained between us. Shielding me from the street.

My heart was a torpedo in my chest, a torpedo with no destination in sight.

Like I was hurtling forward as opposed to standing still; like my skin was on fire though I'd pulled on my sweater earlier this evening to ward off the chilly, nighttime breeze from the Mississippi River; like if I wasn't careful, I'd let Asher take what I'd given no other man, right here on an empty, semi-dark street with music blaring from Bourbon not some three-hundred feet away.

I wasn't this woman. I'd *never* been this woman.

I was more likely to whip out my taser and stun the hell out of a dude for stepping too close, but here I was. My ass driving back into Asher's very obvious hard-on. My fingers digging into the ridges of nineteenth-century brick. My core tightening as though Asher was already inside me when he'd done nothing but steal my breath with a kiss.

To put it simply, I was screwed.

Maybe literally.

At the sensation of the waistband of my jeans loosening, it hit me that Asher had popped the button on the sly. "You're playing with fire, Avery." I couldn't hear the teeth of the zipper coming undone over the strands of jazz, but my brain filled in the blanks with acute precision. "You have three seconds to tell me that you don't want this. You hear me? Nod yes."

Like I'd already told him twice before now, following orders wasn't exactly my thing.

I snagged him by the wrist, and, sucking in hot air, went for gold—namely, his hand down my pants.

Thank God for oversized sweaters.

Asher cursed violently under his breath, his fingers *so* tantalizing close to where I wanted them. "You're off your fucking rocker," he bit out, and then he shifted to bind me to him with his left hand, although if he pulled any harder, we'd become one.

"I figured I'd speed up the process," I said, then fell into a small pause. "Unless you were just trying to scare me, and you never planned to follow through on your whole *I'm-going-to-own-you* speech."

Maybe it was my imagination, but I swore I could feel the thud of his heart beat against my back.

"I planned to follow through." The words came out sounding both tortured and arrogant. Typical man.

I swallowed my remaining nerves and gave him a taste of his own *arrogant-I'm-a-badass-cop* medicine. "I'm losing faith with every second."

A beat passed and then another, and then *I* was the one sounding tortured as the pad of his finger collided with my clit. *Oh, God.* My knees quivered when he pressed down, sensations spiraling through me, and I shifted my head so I could bite down on the outer part of my hand. Music might be blasting but I needed to keep quiet; I needed to be inconspicuous. And, yeah, I knew how ridiculous that sounded, considering the fact that I had Lincoln Asher's hand down my pants. In public.

My thoughts scattered completely when he rubbed that

finger in tight, little circles. Slowly. He did it so slowly that there was no denying that he wanted to make me pay for wrestling control of our hookup from him. Faster, I needed him to move faster, and even though I'd never felt sensations like this before, I instinctually knew that the languid pace he'd set would only get me so far.

Standing on my toes and shoving my hips back into his hard-on did the trick.

Those languid circles sped up, just enough that I couldn't keep quiet. I needed air, and I loosened my jaw as I turned my head—only to have a masculine hand clamp down over my mouth.

"Stay quiet," Asher muttered by my ear, and I could hear it, how that tortured note deepened the pitch of his voice. Another finger landed on my clit to join the first, and those tight little circles grew in pressure and speed. "Unless you want to be caught, stay quiet."

I'd be quiet when I was dead, which might happen soon, I was so wound up.

My belly caved in when I inhaled sharply through my nose. This time, I nodded the "yes" he'd wanted earlier.

His hand fell away from my mouth, and though his touch hadn't been rough, I imagined the way my lipstick must now be smeared, my chin and cheeks painted a blush pink from my makeup.

"More," I whispered, sounding drugged, forehead pressed to the back of my hand, "more. Please."

My jeans were tugged down, far enough that Asher snaked his hand farther between my legs, and then I *did* die.

One broad finger sank into me, and I disobeyed once again by releasing a small whimper. It wasn't at all the experienced front I'd wanted to portray.

"Jesus, fuck," Asher muttered almost incoherently, "you're so tight."

I felt tight. No, I felt like I was being cleaved in two.

My chest ached, though it was nothing in comparison to the way my hips now curled away from Asher—fight or flight. My confidence waned, my boldness slithering off into the dark, and all I could do was breathe through the stinging happening between my legs and hope that Asher didn't notice—

"Avery."

Cold. He sounded so very, very cold.

My eyes squeezed shut. *Dammit. Dammit, dammit, dammit.* "Please, don't."

"Don't what?" His finger left me, trailing up past the sensitive nub he'd worked like a magician, to rest at the waistband of my jeans. "Don't mention how fucking tight you are? That you cried out in pain?" His hand left me completely. "Tell me the truth."

It was in my very nature to defy, but I couldn't do so now, not in front of him.

And I'd be damned if I drew out this conversation any longer than it had to be. He wanted the truth? Then he'd get it, and there was no point in mincing words.

Pulling up my jeans, I glanced over my shoulder to meet his gaze. The blues of his irises looked nearly black, but there was no mistaking the fury lingering there.

I was right—he was the devil personified.

But I wanted him anyway.

Swallowing past the lump in my throat, I broke my silence and prepared for the worst.

"I'm a virgin."

14

LINCOLN

A virgin.

It wasn't a word that existed in my vocabulary and hadn't been since I was twelve years old and fondling a girl from the grade above me in her daddy's fancy office. It was the one and only time I'd ever set foot in a house as nice as that, and the only memory I had of the experience was coming in my hand while the girl's great-grandfather glared down at me from his portrait above the gold-leaf mantle.

Nothing about that orgasm was particularly spectacular, aside from the fact that it was my first, post-virginity-loss.

Shrewdly, I slid my gaze down Avery's frame.

She'd appeared at the club tonight like an angel designed by my imagination. One minute I'd been seated with Josiah Templeton, a colleague who'd heard about my suspension from the NOPD and wanted to "talk it out," and in the next I'd been at her side, Templeton summarily dismissed.

From the moment I'd spotted her in Jackson Square, I'd craved her. But right now, when I felt raw to the core after being thrust back into a life that was as familiar as the gun I always kept holstered on me, desperation demanded that I take her. Avery made me feel alive. With her smart mouth and her expressive hazel eyes and the way she watched me like she didn't know if it was in her best interest to put her stun gun to use or climb on my lap . . . I felt more alive in her presence than I had in my entire life.

And for the length of time that it took for me to have her coming all over my cock as I drove her to the brink, I could pretend, at least, that I wasn't a man leashed to death.

On the heels of that thought came another: "Your ID says you're twenty-five."

She didn't shirk under my stare. If anything, her chin shot up in that increasingly familiar way of hers and her shoulders squared off like she expected a fight. And that, *that* was the reason I'd thought of nothing but her since we met. I wanted that fire underneath me, above me, giving as good as I gave to her.

"I am," she said, her hands at her side, fingers lax. "I have my own reasons for keeping my hymen."

Her lips quirked, and I got the impression she was waiting for my reaction. But I'd spent years battling my emotions into submission, and I'd be damned if I paraded them before her now.

Softly, I drawled, "And let me guess—those reasons aren't going to be shared with me?"

If possible, her chin kicked up another notch. Any more and she'd be nose to the sky. "They won't be," she confirmed with narrowed eyes.

Avery Washington was a challenge wrapped up in temptation, and against my better judgment, I stepped forward. She surprised the hell out of me by meeting me halfway, her face lifting so that the sparse moonlight highlighted the bridge of her nose and the high crests of her cheeks.

"Are you scared?" she teased, one hand lifting to tug playfully on the front of my sweater. With her other hand, she held her index finger and thumb close together, millimeters apart. "Maybe just a *little* terrified that you'll get attached to me after you take my virginity?"

The thought alone shouldn't turn me on. It shouldn't, but there was no denying how my cock leapt to attention at the mere thought of having her crying out my name and no one else's. Possessing Avery when no one else had ever had the chance . . . Christ, there was nothing I wanted more than to mark her as my own. A kiss to her neck, another to her inner thigh. I'd make it so damn hard for her to even *look* at another man without remembering me claiming every inch of her.

My voice sounded like gravel when I ground out, "You're assuming that I still want to fuck you."

Her fingers danced from my shirt down to my belt buckle and then pressed the heel of her hand against the crown of my cock.

A curse sprang from my lips at the same time she said, "*Some* part of you still wants to fuck me, and I vote that we let him do the talking."

I caught her wrist, angling her hand so that it rested vertically alongside my hard-on. "You're playing with fire." Fuck, *I* was playing with fire just considering this at all. I wanted what she offered readily, her hazel eyes burning with desire as she stared up at me. I wanted to forget the hell I'd reentered the moment I'd walked into my apartment to find Ambideaux sitting at my kitchen table.

But, hell, she was a virgin, and there was something inherently wrong about taking that from her. I didn't deserve what she offered, and yet I couldn't imagine walking away.

Letting her give that innocent part of herself to someone else . . .

No shot in hell.

"Do you get that?" I demanded harshly. "You do this with me and there aren't roses waiting for you on the other end of tonight. It's fucking," I said, "and there won't be a damn romantic thing about it."

The heel of her hand inched over to drag along the base of my dick, and, *holy hell*, but my body grew taut. Strained. Heat trailed along my spine, and I thanked God for self-control when she whispered, "Maybe I want to be burned."

For my entire life, I'd straddled the fence. Saint. Sinner. I lived and thrived in the murky area in between, always cautious to keep looking forward.

One glance back and I'd end up dead with a gun trained between my eyes—a real possibility now that Ambideaux had waltzed back into my life and demanded his due . . . in blood.

I stared down at Avery, and squashed caution beneath the toe of my steel-toed boot. She was twenty-five, an adult, and if she wanted a good, dirty fucking, then I was more than happy to deliver. She'd regret it later on if she ever attempted to peel back my layers of police uniforms and badges.

That man—the man I'd been from the age of sixteen when I stole my first life—would turn her stomach. Right now, I was badge-less, anyway. More sinner than saint.

But there wasn't a single inch of me that could turn down the chance to go up in flames with the woman currently determined to light the matchsticks.

It was her decision to push. It was my decision to take.

"Bring me back to your place," I told her.

Flashing me a brief smile, her remaining nerves only

evident in her hazel eyes, she turned on her heel without another word. I followed behind her, watching her six, feeling the noose of damnation tightening around my neck.

Say no.

Turn back now.

Don't take what doesn't belong to you.

I didn't say no.

I didn't turn back to the club.

In my life, I'd only ever taken what didn't belong to me, and Avery was no different.

We didn't speak as we cut through the darkened French Quarter streets, over from St. Phillip and onto Dauphine. But the increased distance quieted the music from Bourbon, and I craved the noise—to both swallow my thoughts and demolish my guilt.

Avery kept pace ahead of me, and by the time we stood on her front steps five minutes later, she only twisted around to say one thing: "Just so you know, in case you're having any doubts, I want this."

Whether she said it for herself or for me, it didn't matter.

The door creaked open and Avery gestured for me to step inside first. The front parlor was dark, not a single bulb lighting the space.

"Third floor," Avery told me, her hand grazing mine as she slipped around me once again. "No elevator."

Our shoes echoed off the stairwell as we wound our way up, my gaze on her full ass, her face tilted up.

Thirteen more steps and we were at her front door.

Ten more seconds and she slid the key into the lock and pushed it wide open.

Three more deep breaths before it closed and I was on her again, like a savage born of the wilderness. Her mouth parted beneath mine, a feminine moan slipping between us, her hands finding purchase on my shoulders.

She wanted the devil, and that's exactly what I'd give her.

"Bedroom," I grunted, my hands going to her tight ass so I could lift her up into my arms. She weighed close to nothing and if she wasn't holding onto that hymen of hers after all these years, I would have torn off her jeans and fucked her against her front door.

Her teeth nipped at my lower lip. "Right behind you."

I spun around, my gaze searching the shadowed room for the door. I caught sight of the sofa, the blankets, the pillows. The sheet used as a curtain just beyond the couch. Something told me that Avery didn't live here alone, and that the bedroom wasn't where she tucked into bed each night but rather on the couch.

I wouldn't embarrass her by bringing it up, though, and I carried her into the bedroom that wasn't hers and then set her down on the queen-sized bed that wasn't hers either.

She lifted up onto her elbows to watch me at the foot of the bed. "Condoms are in the nightstand," she said, nodding her chin in the general direction.

I kicked off my shoes, then pulled my sweater over my head. "We don't need one of them yet." Undoing my belt buckle, I popped the button of my jeans and then leaned forward to strip off her boots. "Get rid of your shirt, Avery."

Hazel eyes blinked back at me before she jumped into motion, her sweater sailing across the room and her arms looping behind her to pop open the clasp of her bra. The black satin slipped down her shoulders, revealing sun-kissed breasts and dark, rosy nipples.

My cock strained at my jeans, and I ignored the bastard, choosing instead to appreciate the sight of Avery almost naked. Fucking gorgeous. Her dark hair, her flushed cheeks, the tantalizing glimpse of her tits.

On my hands and knees, I moved toward her. Straddled her. Pressed her hands to the mattress on either side of her head. Lowered myself and caught one perfect nipple in my mouth, swirling my tongue around the tip until it pebbled, and Avery whimpered loudly.

Asshole that I was, I devoured those sounds and relished how her nails bit into my knuckles as I restrained her. Asshole that I was, I imagined that the sounds she made were for my ears only—and that they'd never be heard by another man.

Asshole that I was, I gave one last swipe of my tongue against her nipple and then shifted upward to capture those moans completely. Absorbed the way her chest reverberated with them, her pleasure so acute, so vibrant, that I felt like an addict and dove back in for seconds.

I stripped off her bra, hooking it by the middle and tossing it over my shoulder. Her chest heaved with uneven breaths, her one freed hand sinking into my hair. Her nails raked down my skull until she was palming my neck in silent encouragement for me to keep going.

Laughter climbed my throat at her show of dominance.

I allowed her to have her moment, sucking on her flesh, keeping my gaze on her face.

And then I reestablished that I was king in this bed, in this room, in this so-called Sultan's Palace.

My hands flipped her over and she released a small shriek. "Asher!"

"Lincoln," I corrected. I urged her to lift her hips, then freed the button of her jeans all over again. Tugged the denim down the length of her legs. Repeated it all with her matching black underwear. "When I make you come so hard you lose your voice, 'Lincoln' is going to be the very last thing you say."

"Asshole," I heard her mutter, but she betrayed her defiance by spreading her knees.

Goddamn, she was a sight. Tight, round ass made perfect for the fit of my hands, a slender back that arched as her knees turned outward and her toes curled into the rumpled sheets.

"The very one," I replied hoarsely.

I palmed her ass, then pushed her all the way onto her knees. It wasn't in my nature to take it slow, and at the sight of her wet core, temptation rose to thrust into her now, hard, until her moans could be heard in the apartments on the first floor.

Keep your jeans on.

It'd be her only saving grace.

But I did give in to the temptation to discover how she tasted. With one hand to her lower back so that she was arched and ready for me, I nipped one ass cheek, relishing in the twitch of her hips, and then moved south until I inhaled the very scent of her.

"Don't forget," I murmured casually, my heart thumping almost violently in my chest, "it's Lincoln."

The first swipe of my tongue against her pussy was met with a keening cry that echoed in my ears like a personal trophy. And I sought out to hear it again and again and again. I circled her clit with my tongue, alternating between hard and soft, languid strokes, changing the pace frequently enough to keep her on her toes.

"Asshole," she whimpered, and I sensed her gripping the sheets.

"Lincoln," I told her, and then drove my tongue into her sweet heat. I wrapped my arm around her right leg, keeping her locked to me, and then rubbed the sensitive hood of her pussy with my finger as I devoured the very center of her. She tasted like heaven and sin wrapped up in a package that I worried I'd never tire of.

With my fingers and my tongue, I worked her into a frenzy until her ass drove backward, seeking more from me, and I gave her what she wanted. My palm connected with one ass cheek.

"*Oh!*"

"Lincoln," I reminded, and then soothed the sting with the flat of my hand. It was all too easy to feel the affect it had on her—her legs trembled and her pussy quivered and either I took her now or I'd be the one coming in my pants.

The latter wasn't an option.

I left her there, my fingers heading south to yank off my jeans. I'd be damned if I ever admitted to it, but there was no denying the tremor in my hands as I pulled open the night-stand drawer and snagged a condom from the already opened box.

Definitely not her room or her bed, and I fucking hated it that I was about to take her here anyway.

The alternative, however, was to stop and call this whole thing off, and I'd take the gun between my eyes from Ambideaux before I agreed to that.

Rolling the condom down my length, I turned back to the bed to see Avery watching me, her bottom lip caught between her teeth.

"It's going to hurt."

I looked down at my cock, which had never, not once, been described as small. "It might."

"This is where you tell me you'll be a gentleman and take it easy on me."

I'd never be that man for her—a man who knew softness and kindness—and she'd known that when she'd all but begged me to take her virginity anyway. Kneeling on the bed, I said, "You should have picked someone else."

A small smile lifted her lips. "I'll remember that for next time."

Next time.

A time that wouldn't belong to me. An orgasm that wouldn't be mine.

"Sit on the edge of the bed." My harsh command was met with a slow blink, like she was cataloguing the words and trying to make sense of them. Then, she moved into position, right in front of me.

I lifted her legs and settled them over mine, grabbing my cock so that I could run the crown through her wetness. She moaned, and I bit back a groan. "You get one more chance to tell me to stop."

Avery leaned forward and gripped my dick in her hand, positioning me against her entrance. "Stop talking, would you . . . *Lincoln*?"

Christ.

I sank into her just as she leaned back, doing my best to go slow, to not make her regret giving me her virginity, no matter what she said.

I couldn't go slow.

My back tightened and my balls drew up, and at the sight of Avery tipping back her head, her neck exposed, her tits on full-display, I lost all semblance of control.

Every. Last. Bit.

"I'm sorry," I whispered, to us both, just before I thrust in deep and claimed her. *Mine.*

A curse leapt to my mouth. Fuck. She was so tight. Fuck. She was wet, so wet and I was on the verge of losing my damn mind. *Fuck*, I thought, as she pushed down and swirled her hips, urging me on.

My hands gripped her hips as I angled for a better fit, a deeper reach. Each pump of my hips pulled a moan from her lips. I made it my goddamn mission to hear that sound again, and when she arched her back and gripped the sheets, moaning like she'd never felt better, I did it all over again.

My skin grew tight and the fact that I was already about to come was like a damn death wish—I wouldn't, not until she came first.

My hand left her hip to circle her clit, applying pressure, keeping my angle all the same.

"Asher," she cried out at the first hint of pressure, "I can't. I don't know if . . . Oh, my God, I can't—"

"It's Lincoln," I muttered, then drew her left knee up, up, up, so that it grazed her chin, "and you can."

I dominated her that way, owning every part of her, exposing her pussy completely, so that with every glance down, I saw the tight way she enveloped my cock. And when she came all over me, it was exactly how I'd hoped.

A flush spread across her chest and her lips parted and her hands left the sheets to grip my biceps instead.

I wasn't far behind. I pinned her other knee upward, plunging in deep with every thrust. And, holy fuck, I burst apart almost instantaneously—a growl ripping from my chest, my gaze hooked on her gorgeous face, my hips losing all semblance of an even rhythm.

I never lost control.

Until her.

I collapsed on top of her, then rolled us to the side.

She sprawled halfway across my chest, then tapped me

right over the heart. "Avery," she murmured, half out of breath.

I blinked, surprise momentarily infiltrating the pleasure. "What?"

"When you come, you needed to say my name."

I skimmed my gaze over her, taking in her hesitant smile with the realization that I was totally fucked. I was hooked, line and sinker, and that wasn't a good thing—for me or for her. Not when there wasn't a damn thing that could come of this, of us.

"I'll remember that for our second round."

She nodded shortly. "You do that." A small pause. "And Lincoln?"

Pleasure smacked me straight in the chest at hearing her say my name. "Yeah?"

"I like it when your dick does the talking. He's a whole lot better at communicating than you."

15

AVERY

"Do you find it weird living in a place that tourists gawk at daily?" Asher asked as he sat on the edge of the bed, tugging his jeans up his thighs with masculine grace.

And I . . . well, to be completely honest, I wasn't sure that I was ready for him to leave. It wasn't that I wanted him to stay, necessarily, but, okay, yeah, I wanted him to stay. *Dammit*, that was not part of the plan.

With Katie's sheets tucked against my chest, I watched him pull the denim of his jeans over his butt.

"Avery?"

Startling, my gaze leapt to his face. "Sorry?"

In that familiar way of his, nothing in his expression changed . . . except that, this time, his blue eyes crinkled. Just enough for me to know that he wasn't completely composed of stone.

His fingers slipping the button of his jeans through the matching hole, he said, "I asked if you find it weird to live in a notorious house like this one."

Oh. Right.

I shook my head, both to get my brain back in the game

and also in answer to his question. "There's nothing but rumors to it. The sultan being buried alive in the courtyard? Fake." Holding up my hand, I tucked my index finger down. "The vengeful brother murdering the members of the sultan's harem and leaving the bodies strewn about the house? Also fake." Another finger went down. "The blood seeping down the front steps the morning after a horrible storm?" I shrugged. "I don't know. That part could be true. New Orleans has always been a violent city, even if it has nothing to do with some sort of bizarre mutilation scene in this mansion."

He stared at me, hands still on his waistband, and his silence spawned more word vomit from me: "People will always believe the story that aligns with their best interests. It's why people come to see me in Jackson Square—they're seeking validation for what they already believe to be true."

"So, the cards . . ."

I cocked my head, considering him. "What about them?"

"They aren't real?"

The more time he spent away from the bed, the more I found it necessary to get some damn clothes on my body. "Sure, they're *real*," I said, scooting my butt to the edge so I could peer over the side in search of my shirt. Or my underwear. Anything, really, would do at this point. "But like anything else, the cards represent what we make of them. I could pull the same three for you and someone else, but their meanings would change immediately. No two readings are the same."

Spotting my sweater beneath the window, I let out a relieved breath and slipped from the bed. *Be bold. Be confident.* Much easier said than done when I ditched the sheet and scooped up my sweater off the floor, naked as the day I was born.

"Is that ink?"

My sweatshirt was over my head when Asher voiced the question. Fabric masking my vision, I only heard the *pop! pop!* of his knees and then felt the trace of his finger along the inner line of my own knee. The left one.

I stepped back on instinct alone, not wanting him to have the time to read the words, and I went tumbling to the floor as my foot caught on a stray object. My arms pinwheeled, a curse leaving my lips, as I went down.

"Got you," came Asher's deep, rumbly voice, his bulky arms circling my thighs. The stubble on his cheeks scratched my thighs, and the warmth of his clothed body was like a furnace to my naked one. The moan that worked its way up my throat had nothing to do with my acute embarrassment for tripping and everything to do with the man who'd caught me.

I was accustomed to taking care of myself, and as I popped my head through the neck hole of my sweater, I vowed to get over this idiotic crush before it swallowed me whole.

That was, until my surroundings blinked back into focus and I found Asher staring at the words tattooed into my skin.

"Don't," I muttered, pulling on my leg.

He didn't let me go. Hand flexing around my thigh, he held me in place. "You bow to no man, huh?" His tone gave nothing away, his thumb idly brushing over the calligraphy. "You get this done recently?"

Two years ago, on the ten-year anniversary of my mother's death—not that I would ever divulge that sort of information.

I bow to no man, the script read in neat lettering. I'd gone to a place called Inked on Bourbon for it, right in the heart of the French Quarter. Immediately after checking in, I'd requested a female tattoo artist, and I'd gotten one in the form of the owner's wife, Lizzie Harvey. A pretty, perky woman who'd taken one look at the words I'd scribbled on a scrap of paper and said, "Yeah, men can be complete pigs sometimes. C'mon in the back and I'll take care of you."

While splayed out on the table, Lizzie had told me a story about an ex of hers who'd dumped her on social media—Instagram, of all places—and I'd nodded in sympathy, murmured my "no, he didn't!" comments in all the right places.

But a public dumping scandal didn't equate to a stolen life, and on the anniversary of my mother's death, there had been nothing I wanted more than to hunt Jay Foley down and give him a taste of his own medicine.

Even if Asher gave me a thousand orgasms, my mother's death was none of his business.

I slapped his hands away, not the least bit surprised when he slipped his grip higher, closer to the apex of my thighs. "C'mon, Avery," he drawled in that rough timbre of his, "don't keep me in suspense."

I could go tit for tat.

Give him an abbreviated version of events that truly told him nothing . . . in exchange for information on the list of names I'd found in his desk drawer. My mouth opened, the words hovering on my tongue.

But what came out wasn't at all what I'd intended: "You jealous, Asher?"

He grunted, then twisted his face away.

Oh, this was too good. Cupping his stubbled jaw, I forced him to look up at me . . . and as he was on his knees, it was with a burst of excitement that I realized that *I* was the one with the dominant hand this time around.

Well, well, well. How the tables had turned.

"Tell me, *Lincoln*," I said with a little smile, "have you ever bowed to a woman before?"

I felt the way his jaw clenched beneath my palm, and then there was no mistaking the way he spoke from between gritted teeth. "Trust me when I say that I only get on my knees before a woman for one reason."

A visual of him licking my core flashed before my eyes. It'd felt fantastic when he'd done it earlier, better than I could have ever imagined.

"Why do you have the tattoo?" he demanded. "Or did you lie about still having your *hymen*?"

The thoroughly disgusted way he uttered the word "hymen" made me roll my eyes. "Do you really have to ask that?" My hand slipped from his jaw to curl one finger beneath his chin, urging him to look up at me. "Or are you about to go all caveman and question my authenticity all the while you don't plan to sleep with me again? Hit and quit it, that's how my roommate always puts it."

"You have absolutely no faith in the male sex."

How could I?

My stepfather had my mother murdered in cold blood, and then had set out to do the same to me.

The men I'd run into while living on the streets had been only too keen to paw at me, even though I'd barely entered puberty at that point.

Nothing about the men in my life, thus far, leant to a positive image now—except for Pete and Sal, and they were way too in love with each other to ever look at another human being, let alone me.

Scoffing, I dropped my hand from Asher's face. "You're right, I have none. And in case you've forgotten, you already made it clear that sex between us was a one-time guarantee. Nothing more."

I patted myself on the back for not sounding like a bitter shrew.

Only, I'd greatly underestimated Asher.

In the blink of an eye, the sole of my foot was on his broad shoulder and his face was between my legs.

Oh. My. God.

It was too soon, right? Was there some sort of time restriction on how long you should give a recently de-virginized girl after demolishing her innocence? I didn't have the rulebook, and truthfully, sex wasn't a topic I talked about with anyone aside from Katie.

And Katie had lost her virginity long before I'd ever met her at the club she worked at.

"Ash—Lincoln," I corrected, heart hammering in my chest, "it's too soon, right? I mean, shouldn't we wait . . . or something?"

"Hold onto my shoulders," he husked out, and then spread me down below to lick up my slit.

Oh. *Oh, wow.*

My head fell back as his hands circled my hips to clasp my butt. One ass cheek for each palm, and two seconds later I understood why: he refused to let me wriggle away from the intense sensations.

He ate me like I was a feast made exclusively for him, his tongue lapping at my clit with determined fervor. And then he made the sexiest sound I'd ever heard in the back of his throat, like he was drunk on the taste of me.

I knew that feeling well.

I'd downed the Hurricane hours ago, but my whole body felt sluggish yet electrified, exhausted yet needy—Lincoln was the sole cause. Him and the magic of his hands and . . .

other parts of his hard body. Desperate to see him work my body to distraction, I gathered the hem of my sweater and held the fabric behind me, knotted in one hand.

Lord, he was handsome.

All dark, messy hair and shut eyes and hard slopes and angles. There was minimal light from the window, but enough of the room was revealed that I could see the high color on his cheeks as he flicked me over and over again with his tongue.

A masculine finger probed my entrance, sinking inside. Curling inward. I was going to die, right here, right now. With Asher sucking on my clit like he was on a mission of his own design, his finger angling just right with every thrust.

It wasn't fair that he could work me up into this quivering mess within seconds.

And when he pulled away to rise to his feet, his height made me feel tiny, submissive, all over again. I whimpered at the loss of him, and then mentally berated myself for doing what I had vowed to never do: beg a man to make me feel complete.

It grated on my nerves, rubbed me raw—it was a power struggled I'd never anticipated.

In the end, I let newfound lust do the talking.

"That was . . ." I swallowed, allowing my gaze to hold steady on Asher's face. His full mouth glistened from my wetness and his eyes glittered. "We agreed to one-time sex, but technically, you broke that agreement. We could, maybe, I don't know, go for another round before you head out?"

He licked his lips, and I gulped down air because that right there, him absorbing the taste of me, was an image that would remain locked in my head for the rest of my life.

Then he spoke, and it went right over me, I was so

entranced by the thought of him working me up to another orgasm. If I became an addict, it was all Katie's fault. She'd encouraged this, told me to live a little, and with Asher, I was all too willing to take the plunge.

One second passed.

Two seconds passed.

And then, finally, his words registered in my head.

My jaw dropped in pure outrage. "*Excuse me?*"

His gaze never wavered from mine. "You'll bow to me, Avery. It might not be today and it might not be tomorrow, but it *will* happen."

As though he'd taken a sledgehammer to my desire, it cracked in two like shards of broken ice. Fury curled my hands into fists at my side, and the blood pounding furiously at my temple had nothing to do with lust. That he thought he could just swoop up in here and lay down the law like he was some sort of . . . some sort of—

The outline of his gun under his sweater at his hip caught my eye, and I could have sworn that my right eye twitched. He might be a cop, he might have a shiny badge and the ability to lock people up, but he was *not* the law.

I'd be dead before I ever let him talk to me like that— like he owned me or had any say on what I did or did not do.

Finger thrusting in the direction of the bed, I snapped, "The only place I'm getting on my knees is if I'm on that bed and your cock is all up in my business." My voice vibrated with rage, my body trembling, too. "I will *never* get on my knees before you for any other reason. You better get that through your thick skull because I'm not going to say it—"

His lips crashed down on mine, swallowing my fight, ending my tirade. The kiss was brutal, rough, and it was over before it had even begun.

Twisting away, leaving me breathless and panting, Asher shoved his feet into his shoes and strode for the door.

"Will I see you again soon?"

The question was out before I could stop myself, hanging in the air, humiliating in all of its transparent, longing glory.

Asher glanced back at me over his shoulder, the top of his face hidden in shadow. But I saw his mouth move, that mouth which had brought me to the brink of pleasure, and the words left me wanting to snag my taser from my backpack and put it to good use.

"When you get on your knees," he said.

It wasn't until I heard the *click* of the front door shutting that I erupted into motion. I snatched my shoes off the floor, my underwear, my jeans, dumping all but my boots into the laundry basket by the bathroom.

I would never, *never* give a man so much power as the kind Asher demanded. He was delusional if he thought I'd just hop to it, like some sort of badge bunny willing to do anything in the hopes of pleasing him.

I'd had sex with him tonight because *I* had wanted to. I'd wanted to feel the slick glide of his cock inside me, and I'd wanted to know firsthand that moment when my body burst apart like a firework, shattering as pleasure washed over me.

Asher had delivered on both accounts.

And that was that.

But as I got ready for bed some time later, I couldn't help but rewind the night to before he'd learned of my virginity —to those tense moments when I'd been crowded up against the wall on St. Phillip Street, my jeans unzipped, his hand clamped over my mouth, his fingers playing me into a frenzy.

Anyone could have spotted us.

And I'd wanted them to.

I'd wanted to feel their eyes on me, to *see* me, in a way that I'd spent the last twelve years hiding in plain sight. Feeling exposed—vulnerable in a way that I never allowed myself to be—had been just as freeing as letting Asher take control. The realization washed over me like a gallon of ice water yanked straight from the Artic.

I slid the bristle-boar brush through my hair, combing through the knotted strands. It didn't matter if I'd savored those moments for the control I'd given up. It would be a completely different case all the way around to submit to him the way he'd wanted on his way out the door.

Right?

It's what I told myself as I put Katie's sheets in the wash and set my alarm to wake me in forty minutes when the cycle was done. It's what I told myself when I pulled my blankets up under my chin after getting into my favorite position on the sofa.

Forty minutes later, when the washing machine beeped its completion, I was still fooling myself into believing that Asher's last command rubbed me raw . . . that it didn't hold a particular thrill, the same thrill I'd felt with my jeans around my thighs and his finger sinking into me.

Luckily for me, I had a long-standing relationship with such lies. After all, I'd been living the biggest one of them all for the last twelve years. What was another in the grand mix of things?

16

LINCOLN

"Is that all for you tonight, Sergeant?"

Wrapping my hand around the Styrofoam coffee cup, I handed over my card. "Yup, all good, Sarah."

If my regular barista found it odd that I'd been in every night for the last week without wearing my Class B's, she didn't mention it. With a quick, red-painted grin, she swiped my credit card and handed it over.

"You know," she murmured, blue eyes flashing up at me, "some of the girls think you come in here for a reason. I mean, like for a *reason*. If you know what I mean."

I knew what she meant.

My wallet went into the back pocket of my sweatpants. I'd been a regular here at Café Vieux Carre since my promotion to sergeant. It sat two blocks from the eighth district precinct, and the brew wasn't half-bad. They had chicory coffee and lacked the touristy vibe that Café du Monde doled out in spades, two pluses in my book.

But the real reason I came here had nothing to do with the employees or the coffee—no, the place had ears, and even if I'd left Ambideaux's little whose-dick-is-bigger contest twelve years ago, I continued to show up here five days a week.

Knowledge was power, and power meant survival.

My lieutenant had an ulterior motive in not wanting to lose me, and it had nothing to do with how well I pushed papers. At the end of the day, I always had information he wanted—and I delivered, always.

Blowing steam off the top of my *café au lait*, I readjusted the ball cap on my head. "You're a little young for me, Sarah."

Her mouth drooped in an obvious pout. "Not *that* young," she muttered, "I mean, I'm twenty-five."

Avery's age.

Hot coffee burned down my throat, closing off my esophagus as I struggled to blink away the sudden tears in my eyes. I'd taken Avery without thought to her age, to the nine years that separated us. Aside from her sexual inexperience, she hadn't seemed young, not once I'd talked to her.

Over the years, I'd seen my coworkers walk down the aisle multiple times over. Hell, I'd even been invited to some of their weddings. When they'd spouted out their vows, rambling on about finding soulmates and knowing, without a single doubt, that there was no one who knew you better . . . Well, I'd chalked it up to be a load of romantic bullshit.

Until Avery.

Not that we were soulmates, by any means, but from that very first conversation, I'd been hooked. Her age hadn't mattered; the way she dressed hadn't mattered. All that *had* mattered was the fire in her hazel eyes and the defiance that radiated from her like a second skin.

And when I'd been cock-deep in her lush body, possession had been at the forefront of my mind, not the date on her birth certificate.

Cock twitching at the vivid memory of her tight pussy, I took another tentative sip of the chicory coffee and tried again with the barista. "How about that dude over there?" I pointed the cup to my right, indicating a guy wearing a black shirt and khaki pants. As though sensing he'd become the subject of our conversation, he blinked twice and then abruptly turned back to the open laptop before him. "He watches you, you know," I said to Sarah.

"Because *that's* not creepy."

"He owns five of the daiquiri shops here in the Quarter." In other words, he had money, and a lot of it. Although I'd venture to guess that only half of his net worth was on account of making liquored-up slushies for tourists—the other half was dirty money. Drug money. It wasn't uncommon for businesses down in the Quarter to double-dip, and Marco Carvino was a better bet than most. "And I can guarantee that he's been waiting for you to drop any sort of signal before he makes a move."

Sarah sighed. "You're just trying to boost up my ego since Tom dumped me two days ago."

Tom Townsend, number three on Ambideaux's list.

Like every other crook in New Orleans, Tom had made Café Vieux Carre his regular stop. We came in at different times of the day—him in the mornings, me at night since I worked the graveyard shift. *Had* worked the graveyard shift. Grimacing, I tipped the Styrofoam cup up to my mouth again, and then said, "I told you, I'd take care of him."

That prompted a laugh from her. "If murder wasn't totally illegal, I'd take you up on it." Chin down, she shrugged. "Humor me, how would you do it?"

I lowered the cup to the counter, throwing a glance behind me to ensure there wasn't a line building up. Satisfied that there was no one there, I shrugged my shoulders. Casual. "Gators, maybe. Let them do the heavy-lifting."

"Oh, my God, that's so gross."

Yeah, it was.

I rubbed the scars on my cheek with the heel of my palm, and bit back a hiss. Ambideaux's little pistol-whip had done more than rattle my brains—it'd created a new scar to overlay the old, turning my profile into something beginning to resemble Frankenstein. On a good day.

Saluting with my coffee, I stepped back. "Think about what I said." I jerked my chin toward Carvino. "His name's Marco, he's interested, and I can almost guarantee he won't break your heart the way Townsend did."

Sarah blushed. "That'd be nice . . . I'll think about it."

I paused outside the café, draining my coffee, tossing the cup into the metal trash bin to my right.

The door swung open behind me. "Thanks, my man."

I didn't glance in Carvino's direction as he stepped up next to me, our shoes parallel on the cobblestoned sidewalk. "Deal's a deal."

The Daquiri King audibly swallowed. "I didn't really think Sarah would even look at me. Honest to God, I'm not some creepy fuck, lusting after her. I'm just . . ."

"In love."

He released a heavy sigh. "Yeah, maybe. Okay, yeah that sounds about right. Between her dating Townsend and then having the hots for you, I figured I didn't even have a shot."

"Congratulations, now you do." My gaze caught on a familiar figure walking down the street, a nondescript gym bag slung across his back. Right on time. *Perfect.* "How much dope is he picking up?"

Beside me, Carvino fiddled with his laptop bag. "Two

ounces. Small run this time. He's, uh, desperate for some quick cash."

I almost laughed at that. Two ounces of heroin would have been a massive haul if I were at work. Officer of the Month, type massive, complete with a gift card and a damn plaque to hang on the wall with my name engraved in gold. But when you were a man like Tom Townsend—or a distributor like Marco Carvino—two ounces was chump change. Hardly anything worth mentioning.

"Listen, Asher, man"—Carvino cleared his throat—"I know it's not my business or anything like that, but you coming back into the fold? I, uh, never thought I'd see the day."

Neither did I.

But Jason Ambideaux knew how to bend me to his will, and if the last week had shown me anything, the bastard wasn't above manipulation tactics to get exactly what he wanted. And what he wanted was me playing executioner to his king.

"Go back inside and talk to Sarah," I said, already starting in the direction that Tom Townsend had taken, toward the back of the Quarter.

"I owe you!" Carvino called out.

I laughed, the sound hollow and devoid of all emotion. *Nah,* I thought as I held a finger up in the air as a see-ya-later, I owed *him*.

It wasn't every day that one of the city's top drug lords helped to arrange the murder of his number-two buyer, all in the name of a female who wouldn't even give him the time of day until she'd learned that he was loaded.

Then again, even Carvino feared Ambideaux.

And as Marco Carvino had personally witnessed one of

my more notable "deals," before I'd joined the NOPD, he feared me too.

If knowledge was power, and power was survival, then fear ruled as king.

In exactly twenty-six minutes, I'd reclaim my crown—all for a woman who didn't give a shit that I was even alive. But blood was blood, and even if my mother refused to acknowledge my existence, I wouldn't be responsible for her death.

No matter how many times she begged for me to let her die.

EARLY THE NEXT MORNING, WITH THE SUN BARELY GRAZING the horizon, I drove back from my first Basin run in twelve years. Pulled over somewhere around the Gonzalez exit, halfway between Baton Rouge and New Orleans.

Rounding the trunk of my car, where I'd stored Townsend's body in a zipped bag—courtesy of Ambideaux —I collapsed on my knees behind the shelter of my car, my knuckles digging loosely into the damp soil.

And like I had on my sixteenth birthday so many years ago, I retched until there was nothing left in my stomach but utter self-loathing.

17

AVERY

"Tom Townsend, Owner of Kicks for Chicks, Goes Missing Late Tuesday Evening, confirms Police Chief Manuel Harlonne."

I stared down at the front page spread of the *Times-Picayune*, my heart in my throat as I sat on my couch.

He'd done it. Asher had actually done it.

Suddenly, the meat-loaf sandwich on the plate before me looked entirely unappetizing. I shoved it away and pulled the newspaper closer. Fingers tracing the words, I skimmed the length of the three columns written up about the third man listed on Asher's damn list.

"Townsend recently came under fire for possession of heroin."

"Three weeks ago, Townsend and Jason Ambideaux, local real estate mogul, went into a bidding war for a 3,000 square foot, Art-Deco property on N. Rampart Street."

"Townsend was last seen entering one of Marco Carvino's popular daquiri shops in the French Quarter, this one located on Bourbon Street, around 9 p.m. Witnesses claim that he did not stay long, but his whereabouts afterward remain unknown."

Dread sank into my bones, heavy and unforgiving.

Not to mention the guilt—if I had slept with Asher prior to learning about his checklist of the damned that would have been one thing. But, no, I'd jumped his bones *after* finding it in his desk drawer, like some sort of hussy who couldn't even maintain her composure around an attractive man.

What did that say about me?

Nothing good, that was for damn sure, especially if I could hook up with a murderer and then still wonder when I'd have the chance to do it all over again.

"That doesn't look like some light reading."

And then there was Katie. My step-cousin. A girl who had no idea that she lived with a sort-of relative . . . well, if you factored in that her uncle was my stepfather. Former stepfather? The newspaper crinkled in my grasp.

Man, today was shaping up to be shitty.

Katie plopped down next to me on the sofa. Picking up my rejected meat-loaf sandwich, she set the plate on her lap and then took a huge bite of my store-bought masterpiece. Her face scrunched. "This is horrendous."

My gaze locked back on the newspaper. "Blame the deli at Rouse's. I picked it up on the way home."

"Ooo," Katie whistled, nudging me in the arm. "Were you with your secret admirer again?"

"No! I—"

"No need to be embarrassed about it, Ave. I mean, I saw

him at the club. Can I get an H-O-T, please? Hot damn, he was sex on a stick."

I shouldn't have assumed Katie had missed me leaving the club with Asher. Critical error on my part. She hadn't even been home long enough to pee before she'd shaken me awake with the order to, "Spill, sister. I orgasmed just looking at him looking at *you* tonight."

Katie knew nothing about Asher, save that he was a cop, and I planned to keep it that way. In fact, after what I'd just read in today's newspaper, I figured the less she knew about him, the better. As for me . . .

"Did this guy ever come into the club?" I asked, pointing at Townsend's name printed in bold on the front page.

Katie's eyes narrowed in thought as she shoved another bite of the sandwich into her mouth. Around the meat loaf, she said, "Hell if I know. It's so busy in there I don't even have time to look at the credit cards as I take them. Unless they look like they've never seen the inside of a bar before, I don't care."

"When the cops come around for another raid like they did last summer, you're going to be kicking yourself in the foot for not checking ID's."

"All right, Miss *I-Have-So-Many-Fake-IDs*." Katie laughed, her blond hair bouncing in its tight ponytail. "Listen, if we get raided, I now have the perfect out."

"Flashing your boobs didn't work for you last year . . . you do remember that, right?"

She pointed the meat loaf in my direction, and a dollop of BBQ sauce splattered on the plate. "Good news," she said, moving her knees so the plate was more evenly balanced, "you're now hooking up with a cop. Thank you so much for giving me the instant out I never knew I was missing."

Yeah, definitely *not* an instant out if he was a serial killer.

My heart lurched at the thought. How many murders constituted serial-killer status, anyway? Two deaths? Three? Thank God I hadn't even had the chance to take a bite of the meat loaf because I was feeling insanely nauseous now, just with the direction of my thoughts.

"So, no?" I pushed again, completely ignoring Katie's sneaky methods at getting me to spill my guts about Asher. "The name Townsend doesn't sound familiar?" I angled the newspaper to better face her, then stabbed a finger at a photo of the man in question. With dark hair and equally dark eyes, he looked like an attorney. Clean and impossibly stuffy. The kind of guy who liked his creature comforts and would never consider leaving them, unless the "leaving" was done involuntary. "Not ringing a bell at all?"

Katie flashed me a considering glance and then trained her attention on the black-and-white image. After a moment, she said, "Maybe he looks a little familiar. I don't know. I can't say for certain." She gave a loose-shouldered shrug. "Unless they look like your hot cop, every guy who waltzes into that place might as well be a copy-and-paste version of the last. So, maybe I've seen him. Why does this matter so much to you?"

Because of Tabby.

Because I can't be attracted to a killer—that sort of irony I couldn't handle. I wouldn't live my life in a cycle, and I wouldn't be blindsided by a fired gun in the middle of the night with my young daughter watching on.

I couldn't tell Katie any of this, of course, and so I fed her a lie: "No reason. I guess I'm always used to hearing gossip at the square. You know how everyone knows everything about everyone there. But yeah, there's been nothing about this and it's Thursday. Just odd, that's all." Folding the newspaper back in half along its crisp line, I jumped up to my feet. "I'm going to head down to Jackson Square now, actually. Get in a few extra hours."

"Want some company?" Katie asked. "I don't have to go into work until second shift tonight."

On any other night, I would have said yes.

Tonight, I just wanted answers.

"I might be stopping to see you-know-who beforehand."

Katie's blue eyes lit with excitement for me, and the knife of guilt twisted a little deeper. "Want a condom or two to take with you?" She tapped her forehead, then pointed at me. "Just thinking proactively."

"What? No!" Heat rushed up my neck. "No condoms are necessary."

"No condoms, eh? If you get pregnant, can I be the godmother?"

Waaaayyy too close to home for comfort there.

Stuffing the newspaper into my backpack, I slung the bag over my shoulder and stepped into my boots. "And on that note, I think it's time for me to head out."

"Is that a no?" Katie hollered at my back.

Hand on the doorknob, I cast a glance back. Katie half hung over the side of the couch, looking up at me while she was upside down. Her grin tipped the scale of shit-eating, and I laughed.

"You're insane."

"Nothing new there," she said, still grinning, "but is it a no?"

"It's a maybe."

When I shut the door, it was only to hear her exclaim, "I'll take it!"

18

AVERY

The last time I'd stepped into the eighth district police station, Asher had been two steps behind me.

Now, I entered alone but with a very clear mission in mind: I wasn't leaving until I had either a phone number or a physical address where I could find him. I wasn't dumb enough to assume that I could influence him in any way, but I just . . .

My eyes briefly squeezed shut at the truth.

Whatever the reason, it felt imperative that I prove that he wasn't the man behind Tom Townsend's disappearance. The *how's* of managing this without giving myself away were murky right now.

Sometimes the best course of action was just to get out there and *do*, and that was exactly my plan as I entered the station, my gaze quickly skimming the lobby area.

"Can I help you, miss?"

I turned toward the voice, then spotted a bulky male officer seated behind a desk opposite the gift shop. I stepped forward, paused, and glanced back. *A gift shop*? How had I not noticed that the last time?

"Random, isn't it?" said the officer. "You wouldn't imagine the people we get through here." Chuckling low, he added, "Tourists, mostly."

"And they want NOPD gear as a souvenir?"

He grinned, his teeth shining pearly white. "I think they'd rather take an officer home, but they'll make do with the T-shirt."

It was the perfect opening to ask about Asher, and I laughed like I hadn't done that very thing in taking an officer home. Minus the T-shirt, obviously.

Approaching the desk, I let my hands fall loose by my sides to keep from awkwardly fiddling with the straps of my backpack. "I actually have a question about one of your officers . . . a sergeant."

Immediately, the man's shoulders snapped straight and the laughter faded from his expression. "Are you wanting to file a complaint?"

"What, no! No, of course not." Although if my suspicions were correct . . . Well, I figured it was better not to think of all that just yet. Innocent until proven guilty—wasn't that the way it worked in the justice system? And I truly, *truly* wanted to believe that Asher was innocent. I settled my hands on the lip of the desk, knuckles turning white with nerves. "Actually, this is going to be *so* embarrassing so I hope you'll forgive me beforehand, Officer"—I glanced at the gold tag pinned to his breast, above the shiny NOPD emblem—"Templeton."

He shifted awkwardly, his broad chest puffing out with clear indignation. "We don't normally give out any information about our officers, miss."

If working in Jackson Square had taught me anything, it was the skill of reading between the lines and deciphering what people wanted to hear. I tapped into that now, moving my hand so that my weight rested entirely on my right palm.

"I *fully* understand why so much information is off-the-record, sir. Privacy is integral, especially with what y'all do for a living." I offered a slow smile, hoping to put him at ease. "The thing is, I really need to speak with Sergeant Asher, and silly me, I never got his phone number."

The man's face contorted with an expression I couldn't even begin to read. "Sergeant Asher isn't here. I can give you his extension number, but I can't guarantee when he'll call you back. He's been . . ." He trailed off, muttering something incoherent beneath his breath.

Curiosity piqued, I leaned in some more. "What was that? I couldn't quite hear you." Tugging on my earlobe, I teased, "Let's just say that I made the mistake of listening to a street band for a few minutes before I came in. Great trombone usage. Unfortunately, all I hear is ringing. Would you mind repeating that?"

At his frown, I cringed. Okay, way too thick on that go round. *Rein it back, girl. Dial it down before you give yourself away.* I could fix this, I absolutely could.

"Just kidding!" I laughed loudly, only for it to peter out awkwardly when Officer Templeton didn't even crack a grin at my expense. Go big or go home—hadn't that been Katie's motto for the longest? I wasn't going home without Asher's phone number, and with no other way to contact him—aside from stalking the station until he came in to work, whenever that was—it was time to roll out the dice and take a gamble.

I palmed my belly and took a deep breath. "Officer Templeton, I'd like to start over." Rubbing my stomach, I faked a hitched breath and powered on. "It's been *so* hard for me to come here, especially because I'm not the type of girl who likes to admit to making a mistake. The thing is, I'm pregnant."

Templeton's mouth fell open unceremoniously.

Time to make the magic happen.

My left hand joined my right on my stomach, and I mentally toasted Katie for giving me the idea for this plan in the first place. If acting politely didn't get you far, then faking a pregnancy would absolutely do the trick.

"You *can't* tell anyone," I rushed to say, curling my shoulders inward as though parting with a very, very big secret. "Ash—I mean, Lincoln doesn't even know yet, which is why I need your help. It was all so casual between us, but then . . ." I dipped my chin, patting my flat stomach. "You can see how uncomfortable this all is, for me and for everyone else, including *you.*"

"I-I—" Officer Templeton coughed into one hand, his face the color of a Ponchatoula strawberry at the height of the growing season. "I never thought Asher would have children."

Since I was going to hell, anyway, I lied yet again. "He likes to say that he can't have them, but really he's just an inner softie. Didn't want to tell anyone that he was just waiting until the right woman came around. I'd say that he's changed his mind, don't you think?"

The officer's eyes ducked down to stare at my non-pregnant body. "Let me get you his number, Miss . . ."

I hesitated briefly, then told my first truth to another soul in years. "Laurel," I whispered, my hands turning clammy where they rested on my stomach, "it's Laurel."

"Right, Miss Laurel." With quick, efficient movements, Officer Templeton opened his desk drawer and pulled out a rather large binder. He popped it open, tongue to the tip of his finger, and began to flip through the pages, one by one.

"Don't know why they alphabetized this damn thing by first name. Hold on."

"Don't worry, I've got all the time in the world."

Would Asher be shocked to answer my phone call? Knowing him, he'd find a way to turn it all around and ask me the one question I'd tried my best not to think about for the last few days: whether or not I'd get on my knees for him.

You wouldn't, especially not now after . . . everything.

In the darkest parts of my soul, however, I feared that I would.

"All right, Miss Laurel, here we go."

Hearing my real name made me twitchy, and I pasted a smile on my face and took the scrap of paper he handed me with a number scrawled across it. "I can't thank you enough for this, Officer."

Templeton's cheeks flushed red at the praise. "My name's Josiah," he muttered, eyes on the gift shop behind me, "if you're looking for a middle name or something down the road, and it's a boy, consider it as payment for linking the two of you up."

The way this day was going, I'd have a fake bedroom designed for the baby by the time the clock struck midnight, too.

Still, I owed him at least my left kidney, and so I played right along with the tangled webs I'd spun. "Josiah with an 'h' at the end?"

The corner of his mouth crooked upward. "Yes, miss."

"You got it, Josiah with an 'h.'" I backed up, one foot and then another, offering a little wave. "Thank you so much for everything!"

Twisting on my heel, I ducked my head and picked up

my pace as I headed for the front door. Pregnancy lie aside, I'd gotten exactly what I'd wanted tonight.

Hooking my backpack to my front like a kangaroo pouch as I walked, I unzipped the front pocket and shoved the paper inside, too preoccupied with tucking it in safely to watch my step.

A body bulldozed into my shoulder, or maybe it was the other way around, and I released a soft *"oomph!"* when I twisted to the side from the unexpected contact.

And then I saw the person who'd bumped into me, and the soles of my boots might as well have turned into glue. My weight swung forward, hands clenching at my sides, and then, like one of those toys that pops back into place, no matter how hard you shove the plastic body, I rebounded.

Run.

My heart shrieked at me to go, to sprint through the front door and hail the first cab that could take me anywhere in the city . . . so long as it wasn't *here*. But my feet, my damn feet were still rooted to the ground where I stood.

Run! Run! Run!

"Watch where you're going, ma'am," one of my stepfather's bodyguards barked at me as they all stepped into the lobby as a uniform group, like a school of fish.

I fell back, hands locked on my backpack straps, my eyes never veering away from the man who'd ordered Momma's death. In my wildest dreams, I had imagined this moment a thousand-and-one different ways.

The most frequent reverie ended with a bullet to the back of his head, just as he'd done to Momma.

The most rational one, on the other hand, had me dominating the conversation as we sat in a courtroom. Before me, on a table, I would have every document linking my mother's death to Jay Foley organized, laminated, and tucked into files that I thumbed through without quivering hands.

But in every version of the events that existed in my head, I never imagined the one that actually played out.

Fear seeped into my veins, saturating every ligament, every tendon, every muscle, turning my limbs into useless appendages that did nothing but tremor. My legs, my arms, all paralyzed. After twelve years, I was in the same room as my mother's murderer . . . and terror gripped me like a poison I'd experienced only once in my life.

The night everything went to hell.

"Sorry, Mr. Mayor," said the bodyguard who'd spoken to me, "another lost tourist."

I prayed for Foley to keep his eyes on anyone else, to keep them off me. I prayed so hard that when his gaze *did* swing my way, it was as though I'd drawn on the invisibility cloak from *Harry Potter* that I'd begged so much for as a child.

I didn't dare breathe as his dark eyes slid over me, lingering for one impossibly interminable second, then dismissed me in the next.

Never in my life had I ever been so grateful to be deemed just "another lost tourist."

Feeling as though every nerve on my body had turned to ice, I swerved on my booted heel and beat it for the front doors. Toward safety.

"Ma'am?"

Oh, God.

"Ma'am!" Clipped shoes hit an even staccato behind me. "Ma'am, you dropped something."

You can do this, I told myself. *Just turn around and act normal, and for the love of all things good, do* not *break down into tears in this goddamn lobby.*

The mental pep talk didn't do me a lick of good.

I looked back over my shoulder, careful to keep my body trained to the exit in case I needed to bolt, only to see Officer Templeton standing there. Now that he was no longer sitting down, it was hard to miss how big he was, nearly the same size as Asher. But unlike the man who'd taken my innocence, Templeton looked at me with sympathy.

Probably on account of the whole baby thing.

Gaze skirting over to where my stepfather stood, I kept my voice low. "Is everything okay, Officer?"

Templeton thrust an arm forward, his hand closed in a fist. "This fell out of your backpack while you were leaving." Fist turning over, he flattened his hand. In the center of his palm was a crinkled ball of paper.

Heart thundering, I shook my head and looked back to my stepfather again. If he saw us . . . if he bothered to take another look at me . . . . Every word in my vocabulary tangled into nothingness. "I don't—"

Templeton invaded my space, palm out. "Take the damn thing before someone sees," he hissed.

The urgency in his voice had me obeying like a soldier in respect of a drill sergeant. The balled-up paper fit perfectly in the palm of my hand, and I nodded my thanks awkwardly. "I appreciate it. I'm going to go now."

His dark eyes flitted over my face. "Be careful today," was all he said, cryptic as all get-out.

Without wasting another moment, I ducked out of the police precinct, letting the curtain of my hair shield my profile from prying eyes—my *stepfather's* eyes, in particular.

Tourists jostled past me as I tumbled out onto Royal Street, and with a quick look to my left, I darted right, away from the more commercialized side of the Quarter with its bright lights and even louder music.

I needed the darkness. I needed the shadows.

At one in the afternoon, neither was a possibility.

Ten minutes later, I found myself in the very first pew of St. Louis Cathedral with the kneeler pulled down. To anyone walking down the center aisle as they roamed the historic church, I was sure I looked like a devout Christian in prayer.

And I did pray.

I prayed long and hard that Mayor Jay Foley forgot all about our accidental meet-up.

I prayed that Officer Templeton wouldn't repeat my appearance at the station to anyone else.

I prayed, most of all, for the fear to flee my body. In the span of minutes, I'd lost every ounce of confidence I'd gained in the last few years and turned back into that scared little girl with her face buried in her knees while her mother was killed just feet away.

Coward.

The word shot around in my head like a slingshot, repeating over and over again with every inhale that I drew into my body. I had lived where my mother had died, and instead of honoring her by standing tall and coming out to the public about what had *really* happened on that terrible night, I had run.

Twelve years later, I was still running.

All those years of *researching* took on an entirely new meaning as I knelt at that pew, my stepfather's face still so vivid in my mind.

I was a coward. I was still that little girl, still too terrified of her own shadow to truly step out into the light and make a change. I was the very depiction of deception, living with my step-cousin and pretending for all these years that our meet-up had been entirely accidental and not, actually, designed by my own hand, after I'd caught mention of her name in the newspaper when she'd made a fool out of herself at an event held by my stepfather, her uncle.

The sound of wood creaking snapped my head to the right.

An elderly lady pulled down her kneeler, and, like me, rested her forehead against the back of her clasped hands. As though sensing my stare, she lifted her head and looked over at me.

"Sorry," I muttered.

"Laurel—"

My weight wavered on that pew, eyes zoned in on that little old lady's face. "What did you say?"

She blinked. "Love thy neighbor, child. You're just fine there. No need to apologize."

Love thy neighbor.

Love thy—

Not Laurel. Never Laurel.

"Peace be with you," I ground out in a hoarse voice, just to return her kindness. Pay it forward and all that other shit.

Sinking onto the backs of my heels, I dropped my gaze to the maroon kneeler. *Templeton's note.* It was on the black-and-white tile, almost out of sight, and I silently berated myself for dropping it in the first place.

Reaching down, I scooped it up and snagged a bible from the pew behind me. I propped it open with one hand at the base, letting the pages fall as they wanted. *John 3:17.* If I were a believer, I'd have a laugh at the irony of the message behind the verse—that through God, you might be saved. Here I was, hoping for salvation or, at least, some place to hide. As it was, I used the bible to conceal the way I unraveled the crinkled-up paper Templeton had shoved at me, rolling it flat like a batch of gooey cookie dough until the words became legible on the page.

If chicken scratch could ever be completely legible, that was.

Letter by letter, word by word, the ink came into focus.

If you want to surprise Asher with the news, he'll be at Whiskey Bay down in the Bywater tonight. 10pm. Wear something nice. ~ T.

Whiskey Bay? There was no way that Templeton, a *police officer,* of all things, was encouraging me to camp out tonight at a strip joint in wait for my fake baby's father . . . would he? I reread the note another time, then yet another time after that. I flipped it over, just to see if I'd miss something scrawled across the back.

There was nothing.

Approaching Asher at Whiskey Bay wasn't a good idea. Hell, it was downright terrible.

But after the day I'd had, terrible sounded just right.

19

LINCOLN

Walking into Whiskey Bay was a bit like stepping into a time portal.

Nothing inside had changed in over a decade, not the red-and-black décor, with accents of gold; not the bouncers at the front door, who greeted me with a fist-bump and a "hell, man, it's good to see you again."

Perhaps the *only* differences lay in the dancers themselves, who clung to metal poles, spun in elevated cages ten feet above the hardwood floor, and were a good deal younger than I remembered. Or maybe it was just that I was older, and probably not a good deal wiser.

Kevan, a bartender from the olden days, slid a jack and coke across the bar to me. His once-curly dark hair had been shaved completely, his bald crown shining whenever the strobe lights hit at the right angle.

He nodded to the drink. "Just like old times, right? You look the same."

I ignored the way he stared a little too hard at the right side of my face. "You're as bald as a cock." Bringing the cocktail up to my mouth, I sipped from the rim, disregarding the tiny straw he'd popped inside. "New look?"

Kevan's eyes turned flinty before he tipped his head back and laughed heartily. "Still a goddamn asshole," he muttered, running a hand over his smooth skull. "Guess the NOPD didn't wash out your mouth with some much-needed soap, am I right?"

As usual when I let myself think about the NOPD and my suspension, bitterness swept over me. I downed a fourth of the jack and coke. "They tried, trust me."

"And failed?"

"I'm still an asshole, aren't I?"

I hadn't meant it to be funny, but Kevan roared with laughter, so much so that we caught more attention than I would have liked. Which reminded me of the other major difference here at Whiskey Bay . . .

I leaned in, elbow on the bar. "I've never seen so many Hawaiian shirts and Birkenstocks in my life." I nodded toward the other end of the bar where a dude stood, decked out in a pineapple-print shirt, tight pants, the requisite Birkenstock sandals, and an Apple watch on his wrist. "What the fuck happened to this place?"

Kevan eyed the customer, snapped his gaze to the other bartender, and then rubbed the back of his head again. "Hipsters happened, man. The Bywater's flooded with them."

"And they all can't wait to go to the strip club on a Thursday night?" I knew why I was here, and it had nothing to do with the dancers putting on a performance for the crowd. No, like some sort of lovestruck idiot, I'd only thought of Avery since our night together. *Even though I'd been a dick at the end.* Pushing her from my thoughts before I risked getting distracted, I said, "Don't tell me the Basement is overrun, too."

The Basement wasn't at all underground here at Whiskey Bay. Dig a little too deep under the surface in New Orleans, and you'd hit nothing but water. No, the "basement" was an insider's joke to those who knew Whiskey Bay best—on the second floor of the industrial building, it was home to everything that the first floor wasn't.

Gambling. Sex. Drugs.

Morals were checked at the door and the only thing praised within were human vices.

Putting his weight into it, Kevan dragged a white rag across the bar. "Same old shit up there."

I took another pull of my jack and coke. "Same old people up there, too?"

There was a minute pause, and then, "Always has been."

Perfect.

Setting my cocktail down by my elbow, I slid a folded twenty beneath the plastic cup. Pushed away from the bar with a nod of acknowledgement. "Good seeing you again, man."

Kevan's voice stopped me, and I glanced back, brow raised.

Behind the bar, he shuffled from one foot to the other, one hand lifting and then falling again on its way up to rub his shaved head. Clearing his throat, he sent me a quick glance and then looked away. "You haven't been here in a while, and I can only imagine what's brought you back. But I just . . . I'm actually GM around here now."

Did he want applause? I forced a grim smile. "Congrats, Kev. It's long overdue."

"Yeah, thanks." Mouth twisting, his cheeks hollowed with a rush of air as he exhaled. "What I'm trying to say is, we still operate by the same rules. No whiskey spilled in here. Not even the shitty, cheap stuff."

The thinly veiled warning felt like a slap on the wrist.

I hadn't been gone so long that I didn't catch his drift, though. At Whiskey Bay, "no whiskey spilled" was synonymous with "no bloodshed." Lucky for him, the club was just my meeting spot for the night.

Zak Benson, Number Four, had a reputation that surpassed him for frequently visiting the rooms upstairs and the gaming tables.

Playing craps, of all things.

Holding two fingers to my temple, I offered Kevan a salute that teetered on the line of sarcastic. "You got it, Kev. No whiskey spilled."

Whistling as though I didn't have a damn care in the world, I headed for the back of the club, sidestepping groups of people as they stared up in awe at the dancers twirling around effortlessly like Cirque de Soleil performers. If only the Birkenstock crowd knew that the Basement catered to live-sex acts, they'd probably shit themselves.

Just as it always had, the back of the club tapered off into a narrow hallway where the public restrooms sat. Passing the men's room and then the ladies' room, I paused outside the third door on the right, the one marked with a black sign that read GENERAL STORAGE. I lifted my hand and knocked twice.

No one answered.

Frowning, I rapped my knuckles on the door, a little harder this time.

Still nothing.

"For fuck's sake," I ground out, frustration biting out with every word, "Nat, just let me the hell in."

The door cracked ajar, and a female voice drifted out.

"What, does the big, bad Lincoln want entry to a place that he *raided*?"

Guess she wasn't over that yet. Leveling my shoulder against the door, I gave a little push to test whether or not Whiskey Bay's owner was still holding down the fort on the other side. When there was no resistance, I slipped inside and gently shut the door with the heel of my foot.

Nat, Whiskey Bay's Queen and Ambideaux's ex-wife, glared back at me, blocking entry to the stairs that led up to the Basement. To my utter lack of surprise, she was tapping her foot impatiently, her spitfire attitude all but palpable as she waited for me to apologize.

She hadn't changed a bit, though her hair was now more silver than brunette.

I cleared my throat. "If we're being technical here, I wasn't the one to make the call for the raid a few years back. The Bywater's not even in my district."

Wrong answer.

Her nostrils flared, and her tapping foot picked up in tempo. "All you cops are exactly the same. *Pigs*," she sneered with a hair toss.

The verbal insult rebounded off my shell without even making a dent. Nat was understandably pissed—Whiskey Bay was her key to survival, especially after Ambideaux cut her off without a single penny in their divorce settlement, which was even more screwed up since he was the one responsible for their relationship going up in flames in the first place. I'd been sixteen when they'd officially divorced, but there'd been no hiding from Nat's rage whenever her ex-husband's name was brought up in conversation.

Those who took Jason's side were dead to her.

Including me, the parentless kid she'd put up with after Ambideaux had taken me under his wing. The dirt on the soles of her shoes had been more tolerable to her than I ever was, and as I faced off against her now, I wondered if she even knew that my presence after all these years could be traced back to the man she despised most in this world—her ex-husband.

"I'll pay double for entry."

It was the opposite of what I wanted, but it was all I had to work with if I wanted Zak Benson in my back pocket. On the second Thursday of every month, the Basement matched the winnings for every other round of craps and roulette as a way of enticing their clientele to keep on coming back. After all, the gambling wasn't what funded the business—the cost of exclusive membership to the Basement did. And if the rumors had any truth to them, Benson had never been able to resist dice . . . or dipping his cock into some pussy right after his winnings from one of the Basement's girls.

As to why Ambideaux wanted to off him so badly—not my business.

At Nat's close-lipped silence, I shoved down my frustration. "Triple, but I get a round at craps thrown in for free."

"Done."

Her lips pulled wide, palm thrust out, and I bit back every curse word under the sun as I whipped out my wallet and counted six hundred-dollar bills. *Ambideaux's gonna have to start paying interest on this shit*. "Triple," I said, just short of slapping the money into her waiting hand, "now let me up."

"Well, of *course*, Sergeant Asher," she cooed in a tone that oozed like poison. She stepped to the side, her nose turning up as I passed her by. "You have fun in there now. You always did."

Years ago, I had.

When I'd still been on speaking terms with Ambideaux.

Tonight, I had absolutely no plans to take my cock out of my pants. Get in, get Benson, get the hell out, get shit done.

Talk about time portals.

When my foot hit the second-floor landing, Nat's voice rang out, high-pitched and all too smug: "Oh, Sergeant! It must have slipped my mind, but our schedules have switched since you were here last." I turned back just to hear her add, "The house matching the table winners ended an hour ago. I do hope you'll enjoy your stay anyway."

Nat twiddled her fingers in my direction and sashayed out of my line of sight.

Motherfucker.

20

AVERY

I n all the years that I'd lived in the French Quarter, Whiskey Bay must have been mentioned over a thousand times—and that was no exaggeration. It was a favorite among locals: the cocktails were good and the dancers even better. Over the years, as I'd closed out my readings with customers, they'd often pause, hands drifting back to their wallets and ask, "Do you by any chance know where I might be able to find Whiskey Bay?"

There were at least five on the map, all dotted throughout New Orleans, but only one that truly mattered.

The one that I was standing before now.

The one that I'd actually never visited . . . although all that was about to change.

The bouncer at the door stared at me, eyes all flinty as he barked, "ID."

Already prepared, I stuck out my fake and made a little prayer that he wouldn't question it. I had more than a few in case one was ever confiscated—though that rarely happened. I bought them off a guy on Basin Street, a tech wizard if there ever was one, and he had a hundred-percent customer return rate. To date, he'd created me a birth certificate and a Louisiana state ID. His true value came in with his hacking skills, which meant that "Avery Washington" existed in all the pertinent, state-wide databases.

I may not "exist" to the fullest extent of the word, but I came pretty damn close. Well, unless you stared a little too long at my records and realized that not everything lined up perfectly.

The bouncer passed my card back over. "Twenty bucks."

Fishing through my purse, I pulled out the cash and gave it to him for the cover charge. At his finger twirl, I flipped my hand over and he stamped the back of it. Black ink, a treasure chest submerged in swampland. How . . . fitting.

I flashed him a bright smile. "Thanks for that."

Grumbling beneath his breath, he motioned for me to duck under the leather cord keeping people out on the sidewalk.

And then I was in.

"Oh, wow."

Blinking in surprise, I swiveled at the waist to look this way and that. I couldn't help it; I said it again. "Oh, *wow*."

So. Many. Hawaiian shirts.

It felt like I'd entered a frat party, and the feeling only intensified when someone threw up their hands at the bar and shouted, "Give me all the booze!"

"And tits!" his friend hollered back. "Booze and tits! Booze and tits!"

I swallowed—it was either swallow compulsively or bust a gut laughing, and I figured the former was probably the better option. You never knew who was watching.

The hipsters, I thought to myself, *the hipsters are watching.*

This was not at all what I'd envisioned after hearing all

about Whiskey Bay's notoriety. The red-and-black furnish-
ings? One-hundred percent as expected. All the . . . I
squinted, soaking up the scene before me to its fullest
extent. Well, hell. There were more Birkenstocks sandals
going on in this room than I'd ever seen in my life.

First impressions: this did not look like the sort of place
Lincoln Asher would visit. Ever.

"You look a little lost, *cherie*."

Startling at the sound of the female voice, I turned and
—my jaw dropped. "*Nat*?" I sent a look over one shoulder
and then the other. Just in case I was about to be pranked.
Facing the tall brunette again, I shook my head. "What in
the world are you doing here?"

My number one client smiled serenely, though one brow
remained arched. "I could say the same to you. You've never
visited Whiskey Bay before."

And she knew that . . . *how*?

For the last number of years, Natalie Lauren had
appeared at my table in Jackson Square at least once or
twice per week. Always dressed demurely. Always a little shy
as she sat opposite me, her gaze locked on my Thoth deck.

But *this* Nat looked entirely different—she wore a red,
evening-length gown made of silk. Her gray-streaked hair
was teased to sultry, voluminous heights, and her makeup . .
. well, "vixen" would probably be the best word to use to
describe it.

Forcing the words off my tongue, I asked the very lame,
"Do you come here often?"

Dimples pierced her cheeks as her grin widened. "And
here I thought you could see the unseen."

"Just what's presented to me in the cards."

"Ah."

This would probably be the best time to stop talking . . . just in case you haven't put your foot in it enough already, and you ever want to eat again.

Biting my inner cheek, I tried to think of an appropriate response to her telling one-word syllable. Unfortunately, nothing came to mind and I was forced to awkwardly sway on my rarely used high heels.

"Are you meeting someone, *cherie*? You look . . ."

Oh, thank God, a question.

Fingers going to the hem of my black dress—okay, *Katie's* dress—I tugged on the fabric and resituated it around my thighs. I hadn't truly felt exposed until this moment but standing in front of Nat made me wish I had even a few napkins to hide my naked legs. Like, a good three dozen would do.

Since there was absolutely nowhere to hide, I forced steel into my tone. When I sat at my table on the square, confidence bolstered my ego and I spoke with authority. Right now, it was a miracle I hadn't turned tail and fled into the night.

Stepping out of your element could do that to you.

I met Nat's kohl-lined eyes. "I am, actually. At ten." The confidence dissipated a smidge when I once again noticed the clientele. "But, actually, looking around . . . I'm wondering if he meant a different Whiskey Bay. I don't think this is quite his scene."

Or Templeton was just screwing with you.

No doubt about it, if that was the case, I'd be storming the eighth district station first thing in the morning with the mother of all complaints.

"Not his scene, hmm?" One red-painted nail tapping her lip, Nat cast a glance around the space. "Do you have a name? I know everyone who comes and goes within these walls."

It was official: I was confused.

Coughing awkwardly, I yanked on my dress again, already regretting asking Katie if I could wear it. As if I'd wanted to impress Asher or something. Which hadn't been the case—not exactly. I'd simply wanted to fit in.

I just hadn't anticipated that Hawaiian shirts would be a much better option than the cocktail dress I'd donned.

Figures.

"Nat," I said slowly, "this is going to be an incredibly random question but do you—"

Her dark eyes lit with humor. "I own Whiskey Bay, *cherie.* *This* Whiskey Bay, at any rate. I wouldn't touch the others in this city with a ten-foot pole."

"Oh."

"Now, if you don't mind, I'd love to return the help you've given me for so many years now. Your readings . . ." Biting down on her nail, Nat only grinned. "Well, shall we say that your readings have been a highlight for me? Always so spot-on when it comes to the business."

Odd as it was to hear someone praise me for what I did, I felt the most absurd urge to throw my arms around Nat and say thank you. Not for the compliment, but for the help she offered. It was something that friends would do to bolster each other up, and I couldn't deny how it made me feel ten times lighter.

"Thank you," I whispered. "Honestly, hearing that means a lot to me."

Nat waved me off dismissively. "Now, this gentleman you're looking for . . ." She glanced my way, eyes narrowed in speculation. "It *is* a man, isn't it?"

"Yes." Cheeks burning, I almost put a finger over my mouth to keep from spilling my guts about Asher.

"And you haven't seen him here yet?"

"No," I said with a shake of my head, "honestly, it's possible he stood me up. He didn't know I was coming—an acquaintance of ours set this up tonight. Told me to be here at ten on the dot because that's when Asher would be here too."

Nat's head jerked in my direction. "*Asher*, you said?"

"Yes." Feeling a little thrown off by the undertone in which she'd uttered his name, I cocked my head. "Do you know him?"

Over the soulful blues blaring from the speakers, I heard her rough laugh. Heard, also, the over-saturated note in her voice when she said, "Oh, I absolutely know Lincoln Asher, *cherie.* I've known him for years."

Years?

Sucking in a breath, the hem of my dress leapt up my legs again—and I yanked the damn thing back into place. The difference between Katie and me came down to top-heavy and bottom-heavy, and I fit solidly in the latter grouping.

"How do you know him?" I asked, which wasn't at all what I wanted answers to. The real question that had haunted me on my entire way over had circulated around one common thing...

Can I trust him?

Sensing my unease, Nat patted my arm. "He and my asshole of an ex-husband are great friends."

That'd probably be more useful knowledge if I had an idea of who her ex-husband was in the first place. I smiled like I knew what the hell she was talking about, and noncommittedly muttered, "Such an asshole."

"See!" she exclaimed, like we weren't the only two people engaged in this conversation, "I'm not the only one to think so! Instead, this entire city treats him like even his piss is liquid gold."

I came up spluttering for air, my entire chest contracting as I choked back a laugh.

Nat gave me a pitying glance. "You'll see one day."

I hoped not, but I supposed that answered my question well enough. Bitterness radiated from her like a tangible force field, and it didn't take a genius to recognize that Nat was *far* from over her divorce.

From my periphery, I watched as an unknown man tapped her on the shoulder and then leaned in to whisper something in her ear. Her dark eyes flicked over to me, sliding down the length of my body, before flitting over to something else. Her response came in a language I didn't recognize, and I didn't bother straining my ears to understand any of it.

Stepping back, the man gave me a single, polite nod before heading off in the opposite direction from where he'd approached.

"I thought you were French?" I asked casually, my gaze still locked on the man's back. For whatever reason, he seemed . . . familiar. The broad nose, the mole on the right side of his temple. He turned, and I noticed it then.

"He has a limp."

"Injured in Ramada in the early 2000's," Nat murmured as though my observation weren't completely rude, which it had been. But I couldn't shake the notion that I'd seen him before . . . that limp, that mole that was shaped like the state of Texas.

Aware that Nat was still talking, and I'd completely shut her out, I gave a quick shake of my head. *Be in the present.* "I'm so sorry. I didn't catch anything you just said."

Unlike the first smile she'd given me upon spotting me

in her club, this one was small and strained. "No worries, *cherie*. You don't need to hear about my parents' immigration from Hungary." She clapped her hands together, the sound like a shock to my system. "Now, let's return to the reason why you've come to Whiskey Bay in the first place, shall we? Follow me, please."

Taking the skirts of her dress in hand, Nat whisked around, the silk billowing with elegance. Despite the fact that the dancers were scantily clad—if "clad" at all—heads swiveled to watch Nat as she moved.

With my back straight and my feet aching from the stilettos, I followed right on her heel. If I gave her anymore of a lead, I'd lose her in the crowd. Following her in silence gave me time to think, too, which probably wasn't a good thing.

What had she meant that I'd see one day? If we'd been anywhere else, I'd have asked about her ex-husband. As it was, I made a mental note to do a little research when I went back home tonight. Nat would be easy to find as the owner of Whiskey Bay, even if she'd never given me her surname. And if her ex was as notorious of an asshole as she claimed him to be, then there was no telling what I'd find about him on the internet, as well.

"This way, *cherie*," Nat murmured, inserting a key into a lock at the end of the hallway. "Asher arrived not so long before you. He'll be just *thrilled* to see you . . . although, we did chat a little too long for you to technically be on time."

Considering he had no idea I was even here, I figured the lapse in time was a no-problem-type deal. "I always love chatting with you, Nat," I said when she encouraged me to take the stairs. It was true, too. She was one of my favorite customers, and it had nothing to do with the size of the tips she left me.

In a world that often looked at me like I'd spawned
horns mid-conversation, Nat had always treated me—and
the other readers in the square—as though I had something
incredibly special to share.

Behind me, her voice floated up the narrow, industrial
stairwell. "Me too, *cherie*, me too."

Planting the heel of my stiletto on the last stair rung, I
stepped up onto the landing of the second floor . . . and
promptly felt the blood in my body rush everywhere all
at once.

"Shocking, is it not?" murmured Nat by my ear as she
swept past me. With my heart in my throat, I watched with
wide eyes as she tossed her hair over one shoulder and
skimmed a quick glance over the room before her, as
though observing her kingdom. "Your Asher, *cherie*," she
said, "is not a man of simple tastes."

No . . . it would seem not.

It suddenly felt too hard to breathe, like no matter how
many times I opened my mouth to suck in air, I only ended
up gasping. Or maybe I was simply panting—everything on
this floor was a sure-fire reason to be short of breath.

Because, no matter which way I diverted my attention to,
couples were engaged in hard, loud sex.

On top of the gaming tables.

On circular stages elevated some four feet off the
ground.

On the bar itself.

And all around them were onlookers, their faces
completely blacked out by the darkness as only the couples
engaged in sex had any kind of spotlight on them.

Awareness prickled like a tangible touch as it danced its
way down my arms and up my spine. When the hem of my

dress inched dangerously close to riding up my butt, I didn't even bother to fix it.

Compared to the women being fucked openly in this room, one panty-sighting wasn't going to be much of a jaw-dropper.

A bare shoulder brushing mine had me flinching, but at Nat's smooth, accented voice, my shoulders released their tension.

"Live sex shows have always been popular for as long as the French Quarter has existed, but with the city council and the NOPD shutting down long-time establishments for dancers just stripping . . . it seemed like the right decision to pick up and go elsewhere."

As much as I wanted to shut my eyes, I couldn't look away from the nearest couple. Hoisted up on a mini stage, the woman was on all fours, a black blindfold neatly tied around her eyes, a large man behind her. He stood, imposing in his stature—especially when compared to the woman—and trailed what looked like a crop up the gentle slope of her back. Up that strip of leather went, to the space between her shoulder blades, then down, down, down, until the tip rested on the curve of her ass.

When the man brought that strip of leather down on her behind with a *thwack!* I jumped as though Nat had clapped her hands all over again. A female whimper cut through the air, and I'd be dead before I ever admitted it, but even my own ass clenched as though *I'd* been the one to take the licking. Heat saturating my limbs, I shifted my weight on my heels.

Nat's hand found my back, and she gently brushed back my hair. "We like to be all-inclusive here, as it's one of the few places in the city you can still find such performances.

Whether our clients are looking for some BDSM, missionary, men on men, or threesomes, we cater to all."

Lips dry, I wet them—and then wished I had a few ice
cubes to toss down the front of my dress . . . and probably in
my damn underwear, too.

"And downstairs?" I asked breathlessly as I spotted a
new group off to my left. Positioned on a bed up on a
circular stage, a woman and a man hovered over a second
man, who was sprawled across the rumpled sheets.
Through the crowd, I couldn't see much of the second
man's face. But I saw his cock, erect and proud, and there
was no mistaking it when the first man leaned down to
swipe his tongue along that hard length, from base
to crown.

My core tightened at the sight, and there was nothing
—*nothing*—I could do to stop watching the scene unfold
before me.

"Downstairs, *cherie*, there is a wait list for those who
would die to ascend those steps. But they'll have to wait to
join our little club." Bitterly, she tacked on, "We're prone to
police raids though we do our best to stay off the radar. No
one enters this space who hasn't already been checked
extensively."

Tearing my gaze from the threesome, I refocused on Nat.
"You didn't do a check on me."

She didn't even blink. "Ah, but you don't truly exist, do
you, Miss Washington?"

Like earlier tonight when I'd run into my stepfather,
Nat's offhand comment was like a douse of cold water over
the head. My lust cooled instantaneously, my brain working
overtime to think of something to say that would throw her
off. Had the bouncer downstairs told her that my ID was a
fake? *That had to be it.* Relief hit me like a sledgehammer to

the chest, the built-up air filtering out as I exhaled again and again and again.

"Look how pale you are!" Pressing a hand to my forehead, Nat eclipsed my hands between hers and rubbed them together. "It was only a joke, *cherie*," she said, brows wrinkled in concern. "After all these years of you helping me, you are welcome here whenever you want." She paused, and I glanced up to meet her gaze. "I find it necessary to warn you, though, about your little *crush* on Lincoln Asher."

"What about it?" I asked, more sharply than I'd intended.

"It's nothing, nothing." Beneath her breath she muttered something, probably in Hungarian, and then piped up again. "I just . . . you ought to be warned that he is more likely to ruin you than to love you. Do you understand what I'm saying?"

Feeling the need to defend myself, I bit out, "I'm not looking for love. That's not why I'm here."

Why are you here, then?

Tom Townsend.

Tabby.

"Nat, I need to ask you—"

She cut me off, finger to her lips in the universal move for me to keep quiet. Behind that finger, her mouth moved, her voice cutting through the moans and whimpers and cries of the activity behind us: "If it has nothing to do with love, then I would like to introduce you to someone. Or, shall I say, some*ones*. Come along."

Leaving me no choice but to follow, we wound our way through groups of people until we reached the very back of the second floor. In comparison to the rest of the space, it was quiet here, almost deathly so. Shadows hugged the walls, and though I was aware of other people sitting and whispering to each other, their identities remained anonymous with the light trained only on the stage.

"Sit, *cherie*," she said, gently pushing on my shoulders until my knees gave up their protest and my butt landed on the velvet settee with a bounce. "They are about to begin."

Who was about to begin?

"Nat—"

Her silk skirts skimmed my swollen feet as she turned away. "I shall send him to you. Enjoy the performance, Miss Washington. You won't soon forget it."

21

LINCOLN

The very first time I came to Whiskey Bay, I'd had no idea that sex could be anything besides missionary or reverse cowboy. I'd watched porn like every other hot-blooded teenage boy, jerking off in the bathroom stall to the memorized visual of bouncing tits and shaved pussies and my one sexual experience in that fancy mansion.

On my fifteenth birthday, Ambideaux steered me up the flight of steps from the first floor to the Basement. He and Nat were on the verge of divorce by that point, but he had too much of a hand in the business—and keeping unwanted eyes *off* the business—that his estranged wife could never give him the full boot.

That night had been eye-awakening.

The next year, too.

Nat refused to let me touch any of her girls—I was way too young, she'd argued, and they were way too old.

Torture at its finest, especially to a fifteen-year-old who'd already been tasked with doing big-boy drug runs for Ambideaux. By the time I'd finally hooked up with one of Nat's girls, I'd orgasmed in under thirty seconds—the slow burn of anticipation, I guessed, since I wasn't a virgin by that point.

I'd never been particular good with looking and not touching, which was why I'd grown to favor the rooms along the right side of the Basement. All that was required of me was to pick a room and wait for the doorknob to twist, the door to click open, and a hot female to walk on in.

The chosen room dictated which toys were available, and no room had the same toys two nights in a row.

Russian Roulette, sex-style.

Those rooms had been my favorite, way back when, and according to my source, Zak Benson shared the preference, as well.

Unfortunately, missing the gaming tables tonight was turning out to be a major pain in the ass. With no way to know which room he'd chosen or even if he was still here at all, and with lights turned down, I was well and truly fucked.

"Harder!" a feminine voice shrilled. "Ohmigod, *harder!*"

Cock twitching in my pants, I crushed my empty water bottle and tossed it in the closest trash bin. All right, so I wasn't *that* fucked, but still.

Tonight was a wash, that was for sure. And instead of lingering around and hoping for a lot of something when it was more likely I'd get a whole lot of nothing, it was probably for the best if I just went home.

Or you could go and see Avery.

My eyes squeezed shut. Seven days since we'd been together—seven days of telling myself that I'd been too rough on her, that I'd pushed way too hard way too fast. Christ, she'd been a virgin and I'd sank into her heat like a fucking animal, with no regard as to how she'd feel after I left and she was alone again.

A good man would have spent the night with her tucked into his body, his hands smoothing over her arms, brushing back her hair.

I wasn't, and had never been, a good man.

My equivalent of getting romantic was making demands when she hardly knew me, and what she *did* know, probably wasn't much to her liking.

If I wanted to see her again—and, God help us both, but I did—I'd need some sort of grand gesture. Fuck if I knew what that entailed. Flowers were probably a given, though Avery didn't really seem to be a roses kinda girl. Chocolate, maybe. Although that brought in the question of white, milk, or dark.

Or maybe you should just wait to see her until this shit with Ambideaux blows over. I needed to at least try and be a decent sonofabitch who didn't go storming over to Avery's to take her all over again.

Dragging my palms down my face, I grimaced as my calloused right hand hit my equally calloused right cheek.

Yesterday I'd walked into a convenient store to pick up milk and a little girl had gone running for her mother, tears in her eyes as she cried, "Scared!" over and over again while pointing at me.

Nothing said "good times" more than sending a child into a tear-ridden fit, and all before noon.

"I've got to go home," I muttered.

Benson wasn't here, and the thought of watching people hook up all over this place while I went home alone was single-handedly the reason why the world had invented the Food Network.

You couldn't feel total rage when you were watching people make cupcakes and fight over whose frosting was better. It just wasn't possible.

Placing a fiver on the bar as a tip, I stretched my neck, giving it a quick *pop-pop*, and then made my way back to the stairwell. Ambideaux would be pissed about tonight, but sometimes shit didn't pan out the way you wanted.

During the old days, I'd been desperate to please the man who'd been like a father to me. Nothing would have stopped me from following through on his orders, not even a case of a guy like Benson not showing up when he'd been all but scheduled to do so.

Guess that was the difference a decade could make.

Plus, making Ambideaux sweat a little was just fine by me. The bastard needed to have his world shaken up some, and I wasn't above being the guy to do the shaking. Put that shit in a blender and flip the switch—

"Lincoln."

Nat.

I was *not* in the mood for another round with her tonight.

With my back to her, I drawled, "Something I can help you with? Or are you just looking for another Benjamin to warm your wallet?"

"So vulgar," she sniffed, as though she wouldn't nab my wallet if she had the chance . . . and we both knew she would. "And here I thought I'd be delivering some good news to you."

Shoulders tensing, I slowly turned to face her. "The only good news I'd like to hear is that your husband is dead."

"*Ex*-husband," she spat out, all pleasantry wiped from her face. "And, trust me, I'm waiting on the same thing. But that is not the news I have for you."

Apparently, it wasn't my lucky day after all.

"I was on my way out, so if you're wanting me to stick

around for this, I'm going to need something more than just clues."

Eyes blazing, her hands reached down to fist her dress. "Then I suppose I shall just tell you this: a little birdie has arrived here for you."

Spinning on her heel, she turned to go.

My hand locked around her elbow, stalling her retreat. "What 'little birdie' are we talking about here?" I hissed, careful to keep my voice low.

Her eyes dropped to where my hand gripped her, and her mouth curled in a sneer. "You have always been so disrespectful."

Was she really that surprised?

I'd been dropped off at foster care by the age of three and had entered her and Jason's lives four years later. Most of my memorable years had been spent as her ex-husband's right-hand man . . . the one not brought to events or mentioned in public. No, Ambideaux had made use of my many talents in other ways that were better suited to running with drug lords, dining with murderers, and sleeping with prostitutes.

And the day I'd grown the balls to walk away, he'd shot me twice and had me hand-delivered to the swamplands.

I was as fucked up as they came, and she was lucky I didn't have a damn collar around my neck with a tag reading FERAL on it.

I tightened my grip on her elbow. "What little birdie, Nat?"

She smiled at me, then, her pearly white teeth on display. "Laurel is here."

My teeth scraped together as I clamped my jaw shut. Ambideaux had always said his ex was insane, and as I stared down at her now, I figured that might be the one thing he'd ever told the truth about. "I'm going home."

"Are you so sure you want to do that?"

"I don't know a Laurel," I bit out, releasing her. "Good night, Nat."

"Dark hair. The prettiest hazel eyes you'll ever see. One birthmark, just alongside her hairline. A certain lightness in her expression whenever she mentions your name."

Back stiffening at her pointed tone, my brain went into hyperdrive.

Did she mean *Avery* was here?

Christ, if Avery had been nervous about sex, this place had to have her absolutely terrified. It wasn't meant for people like her—good, innocent people who were better off believing sex was done in a bed, missionary-style, and that was that.

Guess you fucked up that already for her.

"Where is she?" I demanded, kicking my conscience to the curb.

Nat's smile twisted into the beginnings of a smirk. "Stage one. Your old favorite."

My lids fluttered shut.

I gave myself three seconds to breathe through the volatile hatred before I launched into motion.

I didn't even make it to two.

I needed to find Avery—hopefully before she saw what happened on that stage.

22

AVERY

I t all started out normal enough.

Aside from the whole *we're-doing-this-in-front-of-everyone* bit, of course.

But when no one in the settees and armchairs around me seemed to bat an eye at the man and woman stepping onto the stage, naked as the day they were born, I kicked off my offensive stilettos and sat back to enjoy the show.

Nat's cryptic, departing message, however, made my brain spin like wheels caught in mud for the first few minutes of the performance, as did her promise to "send him over."

Had she meant Asher?

Stupid heart of mine had not stopped beating in overtime since she'd waltzed away, and I caught myself searching the darkness every few seconds for the sight of his approach.

Fess up, you just want to see him *tonight.*

The truth seeped like serum into my skin, and my toes tapped the wood floor anxiously as I waited.

I would be normal.

I would be calm.

My heart gave a shocked *ba-dump* as I watched the man on the stage fit a ball-gag into his lady friend's mouth, the strap going around her head. His thumb brushed over her pebbled nipple, stroking it until the woman's hips swirled, seeking his.

I squirmed in my seat.

Glanced around to scope out everyone else's reaction, but . . . nothing. If people were bug-eyed like me, if they were drooling with lust, it was impossible to tell. *Anonymity at its finest.*

A new thought lodged itself in my head: if the room was so very dark, would Asher be able to find me?

I had to imagine that Nat would tell him where I was seated . . . right? It only seemed logical, especially after she'd sat me on this *exact* sofa.

Swallowing my nerves, I checked out the couple again.

Oh.

The woman was flat on her back now, knees brought up to her chest, as the man lay between her legs and sucked hard on her clit. This time when I swallowed, I couldn't get it down all the way and I choked.

"Are you okay?" a masculine voice whispered in my ear, and I almost jumped straight out of my seat. A soothing hand swept up to the back of my head, under the curtain of my hair, to touch the skin at the base of my neck. "Easy, sweetheart. Just me."

Just me.

My lungs heaved as Asher lowered himself to the cushion next to mine. He was taller than me, though, broader, and he couldn't extend his legs without kicking the stage. He set them wide, instead, getting all up in my space and popping my bubble.

Two hours ago, I'd been ready to cut into him and demand answers.

Seated in the dark before a naked couple like the pair on the stage, I was just . . . turned on.

Even admitting that in the privacy of my own head felt embarrassing.

Asher and I leaned into each other at the same time, our opposite cheeks grazing as we spoke:

"How did you find me?"

"Why the hell are you here?"

At the fire in his voice, and cognizant that we were *far* from alone, I angled my head to hiss in his ear, "Wow, not even a nice-to-see-you? Classy, Sergeant. Seriously."

With his nose, he nudged my face to the side and did the same to me, hissing in my ear. "I'm not wasting time with the pleasantries, Avery. This isn't a place for someone like you."

Someone like me?

To the backdrop of the woman moaning on stage, I cupped Asher's scarred cheek. "I'm sorry, are you referring to my *virginity,* which you took?"

"I'm talking about your lifestyle—it's only been a week and I know you haven't forgotten what it's like for me to own your body. You were nervous then, and I get it. I pushed, and you submitted, but if you were worried about sex with me, then this shit is going to give you nightmares. I need to get you home."

He was . . . he was—

A head stuck between us, and then a man muttered, "Would the two of you shut the hell up? If I wanted to hear arguing, I would have stayed home with the missus."

Like two reprimanded schoolchildren, Asher and I jumped apart, and I fixed my attention on the couple.

A second passed and then another, and then, "*Fuck*."

I sent an askance glance in Asher's direction. "What, do you disapprove or something?"

His blue eyes, however, remained locked on the couple. "We're staying," he muttered.

I tapped his hand, which was squeezing his thigh. "Newsflash, I had no plans on leaving."

"Seriously," the man in the row behind us snapped, leaning forward again, "I'm not going home to my wife so we can argue about how to organize the damn socks again. Please, take pity on me and shut the hell up!"

We shut up.

While I'd been more than prepared to watch the proceedings on the stage *before* Asher had appeared, now I felt only more hyperaware to every flick of a tongue or circle of a finger.

The woman's face was a mask of pleasure, her eyes squeezed shut and her cheeks all flushed. Unlike some of the other acts which took place on beds or settees or pool tables, there was nothing but the stage here. Nothing but their two bodies as they moved in unison, the female taking, her hips moving downward to meet every thrust of the man's tongue. Her hand latched onto his dark hair while the other gripped the rounded curve of the stage, her fingers flexing, her palm sliding, never finding purchase, when he changed angles and her body spasmed.

It was . . . *erotic*.

So simple to put it that way and yet so very accurate, and as I sat on that settee, I became aware of the way my hand loosened and re-gripped the armrest of the sofa, as if in time to her moans that we did not hear.

Asher's hand landed on my naked thigh, my dress

having ridden up. He leaned over, his voice a deep rumble that made me shiver. "Are you sure you want to stay?"

The man on the stage, with his face still buried between the woman's legs, dropped a hand to his cock and gave it a long stroke. The determined set to his face wavered, his lids falling closed as he slicked his palm up and down, twisting at the crown, and my lips parted.

It was wrong, *so* wrong, but my mind's eye replaced the man's face with Asher's . . . and the woman's face with my own. I pictured Asher—*Lincoln*—above me, his mouth sucking on the sensitive hood of my pussy, his hand down between his own legs as his powerful body brought us both to the edge.

And all the while, I couldn't speak, not with that object in my mouth, my tongue resting up against the back of it, my eyes watering with the effort to withhold my moans, to enjoy as Lincoln took the lead and hand-delivered me to a Paradise I never knew existed.

Tongue swollen, I darted it across my lips, and whispered back, "I need to know what happens."

Asher's fingers flexed on my leg. "They come, Avery. *That's* what happens."

I shook my head, unwilling to get up and go before the act was over. Something in his tone, in that tortured heat I heard, whispered for me to keep my butt in this chair and stay still. There had to be a reason that *this* stage, out of all the others, eclipsed their viewers in total darkness and not just partial-shadows. A reason that it was ensconced in the very back of the room, isolated from the other acts, so that to even hear the moans and cries of *those* couples required me to strain my ears and listen hard.

The man on the stage rose to his feet, and, as he disappeared quickly off the stage, there was a general sigh of discontent from the audience—only to be replaced by chuckling when the woman set her fingers between her own legs and began to play.

Without her partner.

I swallowed, hard.

For years, masturbation had been my only source of pleasure, but it'd come with a price—a certain level of guilt that I wasn't supposed to be doing that, that whatever excitement I wanted in bed should be found with someone else . . . and not just my fingers shoved down my underwear, in the cloak of darkness.

Everything in me went tight at seeing this woman so carefree, *owning* her pleasure, rocking it out like she had not a single care in the world. I wasn't delusional—she was here, working, while to the rest of us, we were being swept up in an illusion of their creation.

I didn't expect for Asher's fingers to play with the hem of my dress, nor for the way he reached over and tugged my hand from its death grip on the armrest . . . and then set it between my legs, my fingers meeting the fabric of my underwear.

My breathing escalated, and I shot him a look that could have ranged anywhere from *what the hell are you doing?* to *is this okay?*

I heard, rather than saw, his swallow, and it pleased some part of me to know that he wasn't completely made of stone . . . that he wasn't so unaffected either.

"You'll see," he said, voice hoarser than I'd ever heard it. "You'll see."

He was the second person tonight to say that to me, and I opened my mouth to demand answers when every word in my head died on the tip of my tongue.

The man was back on the stage, and this time, he'd also

fit a ball-gag in his mouth. Black to her pink, but otherwise exactly the same. With gentle hands, he caught her wrist and rolled her over, so that she was on all fours.

Involuntarily, my finger pushed down on the sensitive nub beneath my cotton underwear, and my hips twitched at the hint of contact.

"*Fuck.*"

Asher's groaned curse enflamed me, in a way that the couple on the stage never could. I wanted to hear it again, just as I had the other night when he rose up above me and pushed my knees to my chest and took me with nothing held back.

I stared at his profile in the dark, placing his features where I knew them to be: the strong jawline, the heavy brow bone, the nose that had clearly been broken on more than a few occasions. I imagined his throat working as he swallowed his lust, his throaty groans, and then the breadth of his shoulders as they rubbed up against mine. I heard the sharpness in which he inhaled from his barrel-wide chest, and then completed the visual with his hard-on, which had to be shoving mercilessly at his jeans, begging for relief.

I pictured it all, and I wasn't sure what that said about me, that I could question his intentions and still want to climb on his lap and fit his cock inside me, riding him as the man on the stage thrust into his partner.

Wriggling in my seat, it hit me then that I wouldn't want the restraint on my mouth.

Asher would need to hear what he did to me, so that every whimper, moan, and cry that spilled across my lips would be embedded in his memory for the rest of his life.

Maybe it was the thought of being loud that did it, but suddenly I realized that our little slice of the room, which had been so deathly quiet, no longer was.

I could see nothing, but I could hear it all.

The tiny whimper off somewhere to my right; the wet glide of a fist squeezing over a dick, and a man's accompanying curse that set my ears on fire; the whispers, the moans, the *"please, please, please"* that echoed like a sinful prayer as its owner strained for orgasm.

My fingers twitched over underwear as the implication behind the use of the ball-gags hit me: the couple remained quiet on this stage so that every noise you heard belonged to the man behind you, the woman to your right, the couple seated in the far-left corner.

Oh. My. God.

23

LINCOLN

I'd entered a new circle of Dante's hells—and somehow, some goddamn way, I knew that it'd been arranged just to make me sweat.

Sliding a glance to the stage, I watched as Zak Benson gripped the female's hips and fucked her in a way that only a man who knew he was on borrowed time would fuck. His pupils were dilated, perhaps from the tight grip of her pussy around his cock or maybe from drugs. And no matter how hard he tried to fake it otherwise, his eyes continued to fixate on me, and not because he was thinking about batting for the other team.

No, someone had tipped him off that I'd be here, and had subsequently put him on that stage like a pig for slaughter.

Only, scratching off another name on Ambideaux's list had taken a backseat because—

Her delicate moan reached my ears, and, like an addict needing his fix, I searched for Avery's face in the dark.

The fact that she was here, that she was even enjoying this, felt surreal.

Way back when, Stage One had always been my go-to. If I cared to dig a little deeper into my soul, maybe I'd find the reasons why I liked to watch a couple screw, their voices muted in preference to those in the audience.

When it came to sex, I rarely chose to unravel my preferences.

But *Avery*'s preferences were a completely different ballgame, ones that I wanted to dissect until I knew the reason for each twitch of her legs against mine or the reason some of her moans were deeper-pitched than others.

In another lifetime, I would have dropped to my knees before her—in front of everyone—and knuckled her panties to the side as I ate at her pussy, forcing her to watch the couple fuck behind me while *I* was the one to make her finally orgasm.

Too much, I reminded myself as my cock twitched in my jeans. I'd already stripped the physical innocence from her body, and I'd be damned if I dragged her those final steps across the River Styx and into the hell that was my home.

She needed more.

She *deserved* more.

"*Lincoln*," came her quiet cry, her breath hitching on the second syllable of my name, her fingers landing on my arm and tugging.

What was left of my soul wrenched in half, the two camps battling it out for dictatorship of my body.

Take her.

Do your job and get Benson off that stage.

With another tug from her, my hand landed on her cloth-covered pussy. Her underwear was soaked, her hips undulating against my hand, and there was a good chance Ambideaux would feed me to the gators again when he discovered that I'd chosen Avery over killing a mark.

A seedling of doubt pierced the fog of lust, reminding me that it wasn't just Benson I was ignoring, but also the woman who had birthed me.

She hates you.

Right or wrong, I clung to that hatred.

I clung to it, letting it fuel me into feeling validated and morally in the right when I fisted the fabric beneath my hand and yanked it straight from Avery's hips.

I was right where I needed to be—next to Avery, in Avery.

Nothing in my life had ever felt more perfect than meeting her gaze as I'd thrust into her for the first time.

Now, her shocked gasp was music to my ears as I hooked her closest knee over my lap, spreading her wide. Relying upon hearing alone, I smoothed my hand over the soft skin of her left leg, starting at her ankle and running up along her calf. Teeth clenching, I dragged my palm over where I remembered her tattoo was located, and it didn't surprise me in the least when Avery sank her fingers into my bicep and whispered, "I haven't forgotten what you said."

"Good."

I palmed her thigh, dragging the heel of my hand into her muscles, loosening the tension until she sagged in the seat and I heard the back of her head collide with the settee.

Under my calloused hand, she was temptation at its finest—and there was something utterly sacred about being the first to touch her like this, needy and exposed to everyone . . . though she sat perfectly hidden in the darkness.

My fingers trailed up to the apex of her thighs, skimming past where she wanted me most, to hop to her other leg and repeat it all over again.

Her breathing hitched, my name on her lips.

"Please."

One word, and I caved, just like that.

In the shadows, with the sounds of pleasure echoing all around us, I dropped to my knees.

What the fuck are you doing?

I had my back to Benson and God knows who else, but I was a man with a cause: to make Avery come so hard, they'd hear her all the way downstairs.

Her fingers sank into my hair as I kept her left leg bent and on the settee. I kissed her inner thigh, letting my lips linger, nipping her skin when she pulled on my hair in a silent command.

I was a man on my knees—but I was still in charge.

I took my time meandering my way over to her core, deliberately staking my claim with every imprint of my mouth on her skin. Avery Washington belonged to me. Her pleasure was mine to take, and by the time I reached her pussy, she knew that full and well.

Her hips pushed up against my mouth, my name on repeat, and I showed her no mercy.

Dragging her ass off the cushion, cradled by the palm of my left hand, I sucked her clit into my mouth and circled her entrance with my finger. Her sweet scent made my nostrils flare. So good. She tasted so damn good and there was not a chance in hell I'd ever let another man have what Avery gave me freely.

Mine. All mine.

Her leg quivered by my head, and I slipped my finger from her pussy and set my palm on the flat of her belly. Her stomach went concave under my touch, her lungs pulling in such deep breaths that every part of her shook.

And when she reached for my hand, the one that held her still, I was a goner.

She tangled her fingers with mine, bringing our clasped hands up to her mouth to press a kiss to each one of my knuckles. My dead heart gave an erratic thump at the sweet gesture, even as my balls drew up and my vision blurred with desire.

I—*fuck,* but I couldn't finish this here.

Alone, we needed to be alone.

I pulled away, kissing her thigh once more, and pulled her from the settee.

"My shoes," she whispered, and I turned back to feel for them on the floor. My palm grazed a sharp heel, and I snagged it; the other was wedged tightly against the bottom of the stage.

"Take my hand," I growled, finding hers in the dark, slipping our palms together, "and don't look back."

I was a selfish bastard—I wanted her locked in *our* moment and not sidetracked by the way Benson screwed a girl. And there was not even an inch of me that felt remorse at wanting Avery to be thinking of me, and only me.

It seemed only fitting. Since I'd met her, she'd consumed me explicitly.

I waited until we'd left what was commonly treated as "Stage One" to yank her up against me, my mouth coming down on hers. The kiss, like my heart, was untamed: clashing teeth, bruised lips, warring tongues.

Avery rose on her toes, her hands locked on my sides, keeping herself steady as she let herself be devoured. I wanted to tug on her hair, fist the strands and pull, exposing her neck for me to kiss.

But my hands were otherwise preoccupied, and so I snuck in another kiss, nipping on her bottom lip, and then muttered, "Follow me."

As we neared the row of rooms that had once been my

favorite, I searched for one with a tassel on the doorknob—
no tassel signified the room was already being used, and the
occupants had brought the flagrantly gaudy ornament into
the room with them.

A new twist on the telltale sock or elastic band on the
doorknob.

My gaze locked on every door.

Taken. Taken. Taken. Success.

"This one," I said, squeezing her hand before releasing it
to unlock the door and usher her inside. Snagging the tassel
off the handle, I closed the door and hung the tassel's loop
on a hook just to the right at shoulder level.

Some things never changed.

"Are there lights in here?" Avery asked.

Below the hook was the light switch, and I flicked it on.

A red glow, so common within the old-time brothels
down in the Quarter, filled the room. It turned Avery's skin
to a blush pink and the dark of her hair into a deep mauve.
When she blinked at me, her eyes seemed almost black.

Questions pounded at my head, demanding to be
voiced.

Why are you here?

How do you know of this place?

Why are you so goddamn perfect to me?

I asked none of them, not wanting to destroy the moment of
carefree abandon. I'd ditched my mark, left Benson out there to
his fucking, and, for the first time in years, put my desires first.

Not Ambideaux's, not the NOPD's, not my mother's.

Mine.

Sinner.

Saint.

Cop.

Crook.

Mouth dry, I swallowed. Then confessed: "I've never wanted anyone the way I want you."

With the hem of her dress hiked up high, Avery moved toward me, hips pushed forward seductively, shoulders back. Confidence brimming with every step, she reached for my belt buckle. The hook popped from its hole, and she slid the leather aside in exchange for the brass button of my jeans.

I squashed my excitement, trying my damn best to stay still and let her take her time.

Patience hadn't been my strong suit in years.

As the teeth of my zipper unhitched audibly, I swore my brain might implode.

When her small hand reached into my jeans to wrap around my hard-on, my damn knees wobbled with anticipation.

When she lowered herself to the floor, on her knees, her hands fisting my length, I died.

And when her lips parted, and she said, "You might want to take a picture of this historical event," a startled laugh climbed my throat.

Avery Washington on her knees, her mouth pursed to suck on my cock, was a visual I would never, ever forget.

At the first swipe of her tongue against the crown of my dick, I groaned, a sound so hoarse that it echoed off the walls. She circled the tip with soft, languid strokes that teased much more than they satisfied.

My hands fit along the back of her head.

Her soft chuckle around my dick was heaven on earth, her throat closing, and, *Christ*, I needed to slow her down. Back her up.

She cupped my balls and every thought went up in flames.

"*Fuck*," I grunted, my fingers impulsively spasming on her skull, so that I brought her forward and her mouth opened wide, and that wet glide along her tongue as I hit the back of her throat . . . it was too much, all of it way too much, too tight, too wet, too fucking good. My hand moved from her head to her neck, my thumb pressing on her jaw. "You have to stop. Avery, you have to—"

She batted my hand away, her fingers latching onto my hips as she bobbed her head, taking my cock in deep on every swallow, her moans reaching my ears.

With my hand to the base of my dick, I pulled out from her mouth just before I was about to come.

Legs unsteady, I sucked in a heavy breath and forced my legs to move. Five steps to the nightstand alongside the pristine, sheeted-up bed. Fingers grasping the latch and pulling the drawer out. Foil being torn apart as I fit the condom over my length and turned back to the woman still on her knees.

The sight froze my feet in place.

With her dress hiked up around her waist, her full ass on display, she could have been any one of the dancers downstairs, out to make a quick buck.

But that wasn't Avery, and I could read her emotions plain as day as I took in all of her. The straight, proud set to her shoulders. The shy, almost uncertain way she touched her fingers to her mouth, as though wondering, *did I really just do all that*? The heavy blush that stained her cheeks, although that could have been on account of the lighting.

I didn't think so.

Fingers brushing her hair back, I murmured, "Put your hands on the bed, sweetheart, and keep your ass in the air."

I'd seen the way she'd panted as she watched Benson

move the girl on the stage into position, Avery's hips circling as though *she* could feel him pounding into her from behind, her whimpers so clear-cut and seductive that even the asshole behind us had unzipped his pants and jerked off to Avery discovering what turned her on.

But it wouldn't be Benson's cock that fit between her legs and made her bury her face in the sheets.

No, it would be mine.

Avery planted one foot on the soft carpet, and then pushed herself up to stand. With the gait of a queen, she strode to the four-poster bed and climbed up, her toes hooking over the edge of the mattress as she got into place.

Her ass swaying in the air had my hand wrapped around my cock in an instant, squeezing tight, delaying the release I was so desperate to have.

I stepped up to the bed.

Slid my hands over the curve of her ass and down to the outside of her thighs.

Bent down and slicked my tongue from her clit to her entrance.

Did it again.

And again.

Until her moans were a litany of noises that she couldn't control, even when she bit down on her knuckle and came with a deep moan that had my chest reverberating with a deep-seated groan.

With one last swipe of my tongue, I straightened and positioned myself at her entrance. Put my hand to the small of her back, forcing her to arch a little more. Pushed inside, until I was balls-deep and there was no telling which one of us was louder.

Her hands gripped the sheets as I pulled out and thrust back in, and mine did the same but to her ass. I'd leave marks tonight, red fingerprints that she'd never see unless she spent time looking at her backside in the mirror. The thought alone made me want to reach forward and do the same to her neck, wrapping my hand around there so that she couldn't forget—even if she tried—who made her feel this way.

"*Lincoln,*" she cried out as I plunged in deep, my hips churning, my stomach flexing with the effort to hold off and wait for her to find her pleasure first. "*Lincoln,*" came her husky voice again when I buried myself in her pussy, and then gave in to temptation and gently circled her neck with my hand. She hissed, twisting her head to the side, just in time for me to see her sink her top teeth into her bottom lip. "Oh, my God, you feel so good—you feel . . ."

Back arching, she craned her neck as though trying to give me more room to play, and then sank her hips back on my cock, her pussy tightening. She was so wet, so tight, and I wasn't going to outlast her.

I gripped her hips, then wrapped one arm around her stomach like a band and hauled her up, backward, until it was only her knees that dug into the mattress as I stood behind her. Her nails carved half-moons into my forearms as she clung to me, her head falling back onto my chest as she let me take control.

She felt amazing, almost *too* amazing. Each glide of my cock into her heat was like a vice around my lungs. It hurt to breathe, hurt to swallow, and every time I looked down to see her dress around her waist, her small, perfect breasts bouncing under her fabric, I halfway convinced myself that this wasn't even reality.

In real life, Avery didn't grip my arms like I was her favorite person.

In real life, she didn't let me into her body—me, a

former foster-stint kid with a track record that would make men on America's Most Wanted piss themselves.

"It feels so good," real-life Avery whimpered, her nails biting into my arms, "you feel so, so good."

Praying that I didn't blow my load too soon, I found her clit with my free hand and stroked her into a frenzy.

Her hair caught on my lips.

Her clammy back stuck to my chest.

She orgasmed with a cry ripped straight from her soul, and I followed a second later, hips spasming as I grunted out her name and emptied inside her.

In every way that mattered, it felt like the first orgasm I'd ever experienced.

Avery did that to me.

And you really think you'll be the one to ruin her?

I stared at her back, heard her deep chuckle as she arched an arm back to circle around the back of my head and bring me in for a kiss.

No, I thought. I was pretty sure that, between the two of us, I was the one about to be ruined.

24

AVERY

I could be wrong, but I was pretty confident that my legs were still twitching from that last orgasm. Pulling air into my lungs was a difficult thing to maneuver with my face plastered against a pillow, and I twisted my head to the side and blew away a strand of hair from my mouth.

"I can't feel my toes."

Asher grinned one of his customary half-smiles. Leaning back from where he sat on the edge of the bed, he traced the neckline of my dress with a finger and dropped a kiss to my mouth. "Mind-blowing orgasms will do that to you."

My stupid heart warmed at his teasing tone, and I tried to play it cool. "I was actually talking about how my heels cut off circulation earlier. I still can't feel my toes."

His smile firming, he twisted at the waist and ran a finger from the heel of my foot to the top of my big toe. My knee thrashed upward at the ticklish sensation and I nearly clipped him in the jaw—or I would have if he didn't have quick enough reflexes to clamp a hand on my knee and stop the upward momentum.

"Duly noted," he murmured in a low voice, "Miss Washington has ticklish feet."

"Do *you* have ticklish feet?"

The glance he gave me was all stone-faced, composed cop. "I'm not ticklish. Anywhere."

"Of course you're not." Rolling my eyes, I sat up in the bed and wedged the hem of my dress down to cover up the goods. When Asher had ripped off my underwear, I'd been knee-deep in the moment and loving the show of dominance. Being sans panties now, however, didn't seem like such a bonus.

Searching the room for some hope, I said, "If they've got condoms, toys, and who knows what else in here, they've got to have underwear, too, right? I'm talking unused underwear —some drawers with lingerie just like if you were shopping at Victoria's Secret."

Asher pushed off the bed, jeans lifted to his lean hips. "Did they ever find out what secret Victoria had?"

You were so into it, you didn't even realize he still had pants on and *that he didn't even taken off his shirt.* Funny now that I thought about it—I'd never seen his naked chest. Assuming that this wasn't a two-off type of thing between us, we'd have to change that. I had a feeling he was gorgeous, all sinewy lines and tight muscles.

Shaking my head to get it back on straight, I said, "Well, we for sure know that at least she had some underwear—of which I do not."

Blue eyes narrowing in my direction, Asher's mouth turned up in what I could only call a smug smile. "You can pretend all you'd like that you didn't enjoy every second of me ripping it off you, but I know the truth."

I stared at him, unblinking.

That smug smile widened. "You were so wet when I touched you and no one can fake it that good."

The pillow was the closest object to me, and I hurled it at his rugged face.

And because the damn man had the reflexes of a panther, he caught the throw pillow between his hands and tossed it right back, where it bounced off my forehead.

"Romantic," I muttered, even though I couldn't fight back a round of laughter. I wasn't the flower girl, or the chocolate girl, but Lincoln Asher had me pinned: I wanted to smile, I wanted to laugh, in a way that I hadn't in years. He was good at making that happen. Even better at making me forget all about my vow to never kneel, to never give someone the power to hurt me.

In this room, I'd given him that slice of control.

And when he'd taken the offering, he'd stripped my defenses and made me hurt in an entirely new way that felt way too good to stop.

My fingers brushed my neck, and when he caught my eye, I smiled.

Perhaps the most honest smile I'd ever given a man.

Ducking my head in slight embarrassment, I scored the floor, looking for where Asher had dropped my shoes. "I'm so glad that I came tonight," I said, spotting them by the door. The rug was soft and springy beneath my feet as I crossed the room. "I was honestly a little nervous about how you'd react to seeing me."

And hearing me question your involvement with Banterelli and the others.

Shoving the thought aside, I pressed my back to the door to balance myself as I shoved my toes into a stiletto.

My toes were still numb.

Either the amazing sex was responsible or I was right and the shoes had killed off my nerve endings.

"You never mentioned how you knew I'd be here."

I searched out Asher's face in the red glow of the room, confusion slowing my fingers as I fit the stiletto over the back of my heel. "I thought that . . ."

"Thought that what?"

Swallowing past the lump in my throat, I admitted, "I went to the station earlier today." When he showed no outward reaction, I pressed on, foot back on the ground, standing ungainly with just one shoe on. "I needed to see you and since we never exchanged phone numbers or even email addresses"—I shrugged, then swallowed again —"well, I had to find you somehow."

Asher's hands went to his hips, chin dipped as he stared at the carpet. "No one at the station knew I'd be here tonight."

Oh.

As the implication of that sank in, I thought back to earlier in the day when Officer Templeton had shoved the crumpled note in my hand. I'd been so rattled after seeing my stepfather, I hadn't even given a second thought as to why he'd know where Asher would be and what time to meet him there.

After I'd left the station, I was a little ashamed to admit that I'd ridden on a high for the rest of the day. Picking out my heels, my dress, doing my hair.

Like tonight was a date.

The truth was decidedly less romantic: Asher hadn't even known I was coming.

The hurt came swiftly. Kicking me in the butt. Throwing a one-two-hook into my belly, like I'd been sucker-punched. Honestly, I shouldn't have expected anything else. Sex or not, Asher and I weren't an item, and there was absolutely nothing wrong with appreciating an orgasm and then going on my own merry way. I would *not* feel sorry for myself, and I refused to dip into the land of Pity's R Us.

Not happening.

Although none of this could explain why Nat had seated me with him or why she'd gone all strange after hearing his name—

"Who told you I would be here?"

The vehemence in Asher's tone stole another slice of my afterglow. And, yep, that made me angrier than learning that I'd been the only one prepping for a "date" tonight, no matter how ridiculous it sounded now. Fingers clenching at my sides, I answered, "Josiah Templeton. With an 'h.'"

"With an—" His fingers dove into his hair, tugging on the strands. It was the most worked up I'd ever seen him, aside from bedtime activities obviously, and when he began to pace the room, I didn't even bother to look away.

"It doesn't make any sense." With quick efficiency, he did up his jeans and fastened his belt. "Templeton wouldn't know this place if it bit him on the ass, and it's not like we ever had a discussion about . . ."

Trailing off, he reached into the back pocket of his jeans and pulled out a fancy cell phone. Then, without any warning, he crouched down low, lifted the hem of his jeans, and removed a gun from an ankle holster.

Holy. Shit.

"Hold on," I snapped, hands coming up in a T-shape. "You can't just—I mean, you weren't wearing that when we were . . ."

Asher's narrowed eyes homed in on my face. "I never take it off."

"So it's okay for me to go walking around without underwear but not for you to be without your precious—"

The rest of my sentence ended in a shriek that may or may not have come from me when he pulled the trigger and put a bullet through his phone.

Like he was some sort of executioner or something.

"Are you *insane*? Someone could have heard you!" My hands flew up, knocking a lamp over to my right. Trying to catch it before it crash-landed, while also only wearing one stiletto, wasn't ideal, however, and the titanium stand went right through my fingers.

"It's called a silencer, sweetheart." He pinned me with a wry arch of his brows. "I could have sworn you said you knew how to use a firearm."

Currently, my gun was stashed in my apartment in the cabinet above the fridge, along with the rest of my documents. And if I were to ever use it as something besides a paperweight, I wouldn't demean the thing by shooting expensive-as-hell phones.

"I do know how to use one," I muttered defensively, and maybe, yes, a little curmudgeonly too. I wasn't going to even touch on the *sweetheart* comment. Ducking down, I snapped up my other stiletto and bit back a curse when I slid my foot into it. "I just don't understand why you'd opt to go shooting something that costs so much money."

"Because only one person knew I was coming tonight, and he has no connection to Josiah Templeton."

I wrestled my other shoe on, fighting the impulse to hurl it at his head and call it a day. "And, what?" *Jeez, the pain.* Why were stilettos such soul-sucking things anyway? "You think someone would actually bother to wiretap your phone? Only politicians and criminals bother to do anything like that, and you don't fit under either category."

"Let's go."

Re-holstering his gun on his ankle, Asher set his hand on my lower back. I hated how good it felt—how good *he* felt.

I dug in my heels, refusing to take another step. "Asher—*Lincoln*," I corrected when his blue eyes flared, "you didn't answer my question."

"It wasn't really a question."

"Just answer it anyway."

His shoulders lifted, a tick starting in his jaw. "What do you want me to say, Avery? I'm a crook." He leaned in, eyes blazing with a frustration I hadn't expected, his scars appearing even more dominant in the red cast of the room. "Newsflash, sweetheart, *every* damn cop in this city is a crook in some way."

It wasn't a confession, but I jerked back as if I'd been stung anyway.

Digging into my purse, I riffled through for the newspaper about Townsend and then shoved it at Asher's chest.

"Was this you?" The way the words escaped, I might as well have punctuated every one with a period. There was no room for him to evade the question, and when his Haint blue eyes darted down to stare at the front page with its massive photo of Tom Townsend, I saw all of the ghosts of his past brimming to life in his expression.

Jaw tightening, he growled, "Don't make me answer that."

The heel of my palm landed on his chest when he made a move to slide past me. Even in my heels, I was nowhere near as imposing as him, and yet his feet carried him no farther—like I had the ability to dictate his every move, just by touching him.

I took a deep breath, stabilized my thoughts, and said it again: "Was. This. You?"

His throat worked with a rough swallow. "You're reaching for shit that isn't true. Trying to stir up trouble." He tore the newspaper out from under my hand and shoved it back into my purse. "I don't know how it works with you tarot readers in the square, but I'm going to nip this rumor in the bud."

If he thought I was going to listen to his bullshit, then he had another thing coming to him. "Then you might want to look at this list, because the way I see it, a crook is when someone steals extra candy out of the jar. But this would make you a murd—"

The jiggling of the doorknob snagged my attention, as did a male voice that sounded eerily familiar: "No tassel, huh, Asher? Looks like you got well and truly laid, just like the good old days."

"We need to go."

I looked from the door to Asher and then back again. "I'm sorry, but where exactly . . . ?"

"You got your taser on you?"

"Yes?"

"Great. Keep it close. We're going out the back way."

25

LINCOLN

I hadn't done a window jump out of the Basement in twenty years, but there was no time like the present.

When your choices came down to scaling a building or walking into a bullet, there was only one option: out the window we went.

Unlatching the window, I slid the plaster sill up and thanked God that Nat hadn't moved from the French Quarter into a nineteenth-century residence. No, Whiskey Bay could be found in an old cereal-making factory, and the windows were both tall and wide. I shoved it up, leveraging my shoulder beneath its weight so I could re-hinge the latch.

Then I turned to Avery, my palm held out.

"This is the 'back way'?" she asked, and I didn't miss the way her voice hitched on the word. She was nervous, and I understood that, but there was only one reason why Josiah Templeton would have teamed up with someone who wasn't the NOPD, and that meant my ass was on the line.

And because I'd been idiot enough to get caught almost-kissing her against the precinct, now my old boss believed that Avery meant something to me. Collateral, at its finest.

I just wished I hadn't been so blind tonight to see that it'd all been a setup.

The craps table winnings being doled out an hour earlier.

Zak Benson on Stage One, instead of seated at the gaming tables.

Nat rushing me to sit with Avery, when she hated my guts with every fiber of her being . . . and had never, not once, lifted a finger to help me in my entire life.

Laurel.

The name sprung to mind, and I shoved it away. We had to go—*now.*

I swung my arm around Avery's waist, hauling her onto the windowsill. "Move your legs there," I instructed, pointing to the fire stairwell just three feet beneath the ledge.

When she spoke, her voice was ten layers of annoyed. "You let me believe we were literally jumping out of this window."

"It was a joke."

"You don't make jokes," she quipped, dropping her feet onto the platform.

Eyeing the door to the room—and hearing Templeton calling my name—I followed her through and slammed the window shut. "Seemed like a good time to start," I muttered, angling her so that she could file through the narrow path that led us down along the building, some forty feet up in the air.

Her gait incredibly uneven, she tossed back, "I'm pretty sure I liked you more when you were all brooding and surly."

"Don't worry, that Lincoln will be back soon enough and then you'll remember how much you prefer me cracking jokes."

"Just in time for you to kill someone off that list of yours."

Hearing the fury in her tone, I snapped, "What the hell are you even talking about?"

At the end of the building, we turned down, stepping onto the circular stairwell that would lead us to a small, grassy bank just next to the Mississippi River. *If it's even still there.* Christ, if it wasn't—if the river had assumed that spot of land—we were screwed in every meaning of the word.

Avery's stilettos echoed like pin drops with each wobbly step she took. "Your *list*. Josef Banterelli—dead. Micah Welsh—dead. Tom Townsend, missing."

I stared at the back of her head, my heart pumping blood that seemed to skip my head completely and head straight south to my legs. They were frozen, unable to move, and I snaked out a hand to grind Avery to a stop, too.

Her right arm flung backward as she turned to me, her nostrils flaring. A second later, her precious taser was trained on me—aimed right at my crotch. "*Don't* touch me."

On anyone else, that might have worked.

On me, she didn't stand a chance.

I gripped her wrist, popped the taser free, and dropped the damn thing over the side of the stairwell.

It took ten seconds for me to hear the *plop!* of it hitting muddy river water.

Only a second after that for Avery to lose her ever-lovin' mind.

"Are you *insane*?" she hissed for the second time tonight. "You tell me to keep that on me and then you . . . you—"

With sharp jabbing motions, she gestured to where it'd fallen below. "That! You did that!"

I hooked a hand on her shoulder, turning her back around, and began to march her down the metal steps. "It was safer than you shooting me with it."

"Says who? *You*?"

"You're fucked without me, sweetheart. What are you going to do, tell Templeton and his lackeys to hold off a second while you wait for a cab to drive you home? Because, yeah, that's going to go over real well."

Her silence was a personal win, until she cut back with: "Because your car is going to work any better? Like they don't have it completely swarmed already?"

"Ah," I murmured, my tone laced with sarcasm, "but I didn't park in the lot with everyone else."

Shoulders twitching under my hands, she glanced back at me. "Was Zak Benson here tonight?" Her gaze was steady as she waited for my answer, and I had a feeling that no matter which way I answered this for her, she was going to be disappointed.

Surprise trickled down at my spine as I remembered what Ambideaux had told me—about how he'd stashed another list in my desk drawer as a way to incriminate me if needed.

Apparently, Avery Washington had filched it when she'd been in my office the other night.

If I weren't so furious, I'd applaud her.

As it was, I just wanted to keep us both safe long enough that we could hash this out somewhere else.

"Number four," she said, a little more forceful this time, "was Zak Benson here tonight?"

I didn't know what possessed me to tell the truth when I so rarely did in my life. Maybe it was the way she stared at me or maybe it was that I was so damn tired of the lies and everything else. Either way, as soon as I opened my mouth, I should have known it'd be a big mistake:

"He was the guy on Stage One. The one we watched for close to an hour."

26

AVERY

Betrayal was such a funny emotion.

You could dole it out in spades, never batting an eye as you cut someone to the quick.

But the minute it turned your way, exposing your weaknesses and highlighting your insecurities—well, suddenly, it seemed like something you'd never recover from.

I tore my gaze from Asher, away from the inscrutable expression on his face, and continued down the stairwell.

Why are you even upset right now? You knew all this going in.

I'd suspected but I hadn't known for certain.

Turns out, hearing the confirmation wasn't what I'd wanted to hear at all.

And if he'd been here for Zak Benson tonight—no matter that he'd spent time with me instead—that meant that Tabby was up next. I couldn't let that happen.

My fingers twitched, missing the option to yank my taser out of my purse and put it to good use. Without it, I felt vulnerable, weak, and when Asher put his hand on my shoulder to draw me to a stop, I wondered if I could trust him at all . . . or if this was part of some bigger plan to toss me to the wolves.

"Let me go first," he muttered, stepping around me. "It's a ten-foot drop to the grass and you'll break an ankle if you attempt it."

"You sound like you've done this a time or two before."

Blue eyes touched on my face as he turned his body and gripped the base of the fire stairwell. "From the age of fifteen to sixteen, I was allowed upstairs but was never given permission to enter the rooms. How do you think I learned this stairwell even existed?"

His body went into freefall before I had the chance to respond. Heart sinking, I lurched forward, hands on the railing, to see him land in a body roll in the grass below.

I hate how sexy that was.

Climbing to his feet, he motioned for me to jump.

I looked down at my heels.

They were going to have to go.

In record time, I'd stripped them both off and threw them overboard.

There was a *plunk!* of a heel hitting the water, and then a denser *thud* sound, like it'd landed on the ground below.

I guess it was a good thing I'd decided that I hated them after all these hours.

Positioning myself just like Asher had, ass out to the wind, I took a deep, steadying breath. "You can do this," I whispered to myself.

"I got you, Avery," came Asher's voice below. "It's not far from you to me."

I'd spent most of my life watching out for myself, and it was no different now. If I survived tonight, it'd be because I stayed on top of my game and trusted no one.

Not even Lincoln Asher.

The thought twisted my stomach, and I chose that moment to push free.

My body fell, dropping, dropping, dropping, the cool air rushing up under my dress and hitting my panty-less crotch—

Sturdy, masculine arms caught me, dragging me inward and keeping me close.

"Brave girl," he whispered against my hairline, and I tried, I tried so hard not to melt at the words.

I was brave.

I'd always been brave.

Lincoln Asher didn't know the half of it.

"Can you run with no shoes?"

"I've done worse," I told him, and I could see it in the firm line of his mouth. He wanted to ask questions. He wanted answers.

What happened tonight wouldn't happen again, though.

I'd survived this long by staying cautious, and Asher had slipped under all of that when I'd least expected it. He was dangerous . . . and it wasn't simply because he'd murdered.

His hand wrapped around mine, tugging me behind him.

The soil was damp from being so close to the river, and my toes squished every time they hit the ground with another step.

We could have run for an hour. We could have run for only ten minutes.

The darkness was a thief stealing time, and it was only when Asher slowed, disengaging our handhold, that I felt myself breathe a little easier. The field ahead was blessedly empty, aside from one SUV so far off to the right that it was nearly concealed in a thicket of cypress trees.

"Take this."

I glanced at him, shock no doubt written across my face as he held out his gun. "I-I—"

"You're getting some life lessons today," he drawled, shoving the pistol into my hand and slipping my finger over the trigger guard. "Don't touch the trigger unless you actually plan to shoot. Goes without saying—don't shoot at me." Then, he bent down and pulled another gun from his left ankle.

The man was a dispensary for guns.

It would be obscene if it wasn't so sexy.

No, not *sexy.*

"Is the SUV yours?" I asked, fondling the gun like I knew what the hell I was doing.

"Yup." He glanced over at me. "You can yell at me and pretend to shoot me once we're way out of here. Until then . . . stick behind me and don't say a word."

I followed his order, biting my lip to keep from mouthing off.

In the far distance, I could almost hear the notes of jazz playing. Closer up, there was the gentle rush of the Mississippi River lapping up against the levees. Beneath me, my bare feet shuffled through the short grass.

Watching Asher as we approached the SUV was like something out of a movie. He dropped to his knees and checked beneath the car. Flicked on the light attached to his pistol and peered into every window. Only when he gave me a nod of approval did we hop inside.

He started the ignition, put the SUV in drive, and peeled out of the vacant field as though the bats of hell, themselves, were chasing us down.

"You're not trembling," he muttered a few minutes later when we pulled up to a red light. "I figured you'd be shaken to the core."

I was, but I wouldn't let him see it.

"I think I'll honestly just feel better after putting on some underwear."

That made him laugh, and it was such a nice, deep, reassuring sound that I joined in. The laughter spread like wildfire between us, until we were going at it so hard that the car behind beeped to get us moving when the traffic light switched to green.

The giggle monster, my momma had always called it. *When you're scared and relieved all at the same time, you'll laugh until you die.*

Maybe I would.

Maybe it'd be better that way, to at least know that the laughter was better than the tears.

When we pulled up at the next red light, the laughter was gone.

I turned to him, determined to make him open up about his plans for Tabby, only to see the barrel of a gun staring back.

And Asher wasn't the one holding it.

A whimper escaped my lips, and I peered up to see a matching pistol positioned beneath Asher's jawline.

"Well, if I haven't just stumbled right into a little family reunion," said a voice from the backseat of the car, "the spawn of our lovely city mayor. Or should I say, his bastard son and long-lost stepdaughter. How utterly *quaint*."

To Be Continued in DEFIED, Book 2 of the Blood Duet...

DEAR FABULOUS READER

Hi there! I so hope you enjoyed *SWORN*, and if you are new to my books, welcome to the family!

In the back of all my books, I always love to include a Dear Reader section that talks about what locations from the book can be visited in real life or what sparked my inspiration for a particular plot point.

We'll break it down bullet-point style :)

- The Sultan's Palace where Avery and Katie live is...real! But, much like in *SWORN*, the story is very much spun of tall tales and rumors. As the legend goes, a man arrived at the port of New Orleans around the 1860s and immediately rented out the property at Dauphine and Orleans from a well-to-do gentleman. Some months later, a ship arrived in the port and it took a full *week* for everyone to disembark and make the four-block trek to the house from the docks. Arriving from somewhere in the Middle East, it was a sultan, his harem, and his bodyguards. Once they entered the house, no one was ever seen coming or going until one night, some many months later, when a storm ravaged the city. The next morning, a little boy was running down the street when he caught sight of a trickle of blood leading down the front steps. He rushed to the police precinct, and they all hurried over. Opening the door, what they found turned their stomachs. There was the metallic scent of blood in the air and there were bodies strewn this way and that, all decapitated. They went to the courtyard in search of the sultan, and while the soil was still soggy from the night before, they found him there, his one hand reaching out from the ground, where he'd been buried alive. Who did it? Well, they say it was the first man who'd arrived in the city, perhaps the sultan's brother who'd orchestrated the whole thing, and who was jealous of all the riches his brother had....PHEW. That was dramatic, am I right? And all untrue, but it makes for a great story and I couldn't resist using it as the backdrop for Avery's apartment. It is actually an apartment building today, and thanks to some lovely condo owners who let me in while I was a tour guide, I can say that it's quite beautiful! But, yep, definitely not the stage of a horrific scene as the stories go! If you are keen to learn more, a quick search of "Sultan's Palace New Orleans" will bring it right up for you!

- Mr. Luis and I like to joke around that between the two of us, we have all the shadowy parts of New Orleans covered. Him as a police officer for the city, and me, as a former tour guide for a ghost tour company. When beginning *SWORN*, I became (rather) obsessed with the idea of a book that played in on inner-city politics, quietly hushed events involving our finest men in blue, and the local lore that is so intrinsically *New Orleans* that it can't be separated without causing a loss to the city's culture. New Orleans has been my home for over a decade, and it carries a torch of vitality that anyone who has ever lived here will just say, "Yep, that's New Orleans for you." We are a city of people that loves our history, and here are a few ways I pulled that all in to *SWORN*:

- Tarot readers in Jackson Square—aside from my mother reading Tarot and so having a special place in my heart, I truly wanted to bring this somewhat "otherworldly" feel into *SWORN*. The readers in Jackson Square are staples of the French Quarter, but they've had their rough patches with city ordinances cracking down on them, enforcing permits and times in which they can operate. Moreover, I wanted to show that Tarot isn't an "evil" thing, and like Avery showed us—it's all in the way the cards are read. Poor Lincoln! ;)

- The Atchafalaya Basin, also known as "Whiskey Bay"—the Basin has long since been a spot for, unfortunately, crime. Check online and you'll find article after article about bodies popping up. But what really interested me was the case of Baton Rouge's serial killer [name redacted here but can be found online] dating to the early

2000's. In fact, there were *two* serial killers operating at the same time in the same areas, though they had no known links to each other. Many of the victims were found in their homes, but a few were discovered at the base of the bridge of the Basin. When it came to Ambideaux, it felt important that he teeter the line of respectability—and, more specifically, that everything he did was calculated and methodical. A drive out to Whiskey Bay, and therefore seeming "innocent" of any of the people disappearing from New Orleans, fit his profile. Even so, I had to include the term "Whiskey Bay" somehow, and I hope Nat would approve.

- Sex and New Orleans go hand-in-hand. Home to Gallatin Street, a nineteenth-century strip of seven or so blocks that would make anyone quiver in their boots, it was once said that if you could make it on Gallatin, you could make it anywhere in the world. Fast-forward some forty years, and you'd find yourself smack-dub in the middle of the Storyville era, which was a quarantined section within the French Quarter that allowed all brothels to operate without penalty. Naturally, if you operated *outside* of that area in the Quarter, you'd be shut down immediately. Storyville produced Louis Armstrong—okay, well, he was born there and got his start there—and was the first legalized red light district in the country with some of the madams (i.e. Josie Arlington) making so much money that they mingled with politicians on the regular, owned some of the finest homes in the city, and were take-charge businesswomen, despite the unfortunate business they operated in. The Basement is my little nod to that era in time, which has always fascinated me. And I have to imagine that if Nat had lived at the turn of the century, she would have given any of those ladies a run for their money. Literally!

Although there are many others, I may have rambled long enough! LOL! If you're thinking to yourself, "*Did this happen in real life, Maria?*" Always feel free to reach out. I'm happy to talk New Orleans, and generally speaking, scandalous activities are my favorite discussion topics when it comes to history :)

Xoxo,

Maria

ACKNOWLEDGEMENTS

I can't even begin to express all of my thank-you's for *SWORN*. For almost a year now, I have had Lincoln and Avery on the brain, always there, always waiting, to have their story told.

It wasn't like any of my other books—it was raw and twisted and in possession of a wild story. It knocked me on my butt (multiple times) and was single-handedly the reason why my house existed in chaos for weeks at a time when I couldn't bear to rip myself away from my laptop.

Never have I been quite so obsessed with a book or a couple as I am with Lincoln and Avery, and so thank you from the bottom of my heart for picking up this book and giving it a try. It means more to me than you will ever know.

As always, this book wouldn't have been possible without my amazing team:

-Najla, girl, you continue to rock my world with each book cover, but I'm not kidding when I say that *SWORN* and *DEFIED* have stolen the show. You are amazing!

- Kathy, I would be lost without you. Lost and wandering, and I will say this over and over again, but I could not be on this journey without your expertise, guidance, and patience. Thank you for putting up with me when I'm struggling, a general hot mess, and vowing to make you T-shirts. Which will happen - I promise.

- Tandy, thank you for making this book shine! I'm so glad we're coming up on our one-year publiversary soon. Celebrations all the way around!

- Tina, thank you for keeping my butt on track, for sending me texts just checking to make sure I'm still alive, and for being the best right-hand woman a girl could ever ask for. I love ya, lady.

- To my beta readers, Brenda and Viper - thank you! Thank you so much for reading my words before anyone else, for your endless support, and for easing my nerves when they spiral out of control. I'm so thankful to have met both of you.

- To my VIPers, y'all are the foundation of my career. This author business wouldn't be possible without you, and I'm so lucky to have you all on this journey with me.

- BBA: YOU GIRLS ROCK. Yes, caps were necessary. Y'all are my safe place, my rock. I love our Hangout + Wine Sessions, and our love of books, and I love, more than anything, that we are a family. Thank you for being the first ones to show Lincoln & Avery some love back in 2017. If you think about it, this book wouldn't even exist without you!

- To every blogger, reviewer, or reader who passed on word about *SWORN* and told your friends about this book or took the time to write a review, I can never say thank you enough.

- And to *you*, Dear Reader, thank you for making my author dream a reality. Thank you for taking a chance on my words. And I promise, all the questions you have will be answered in *DEFIED.*

Much love,

Maria Luis

SNEAK PEEK OF SAY YOU'LL BE MINE

Love hot cops *and* New Orleans? Oh, and you love to laugh? Perfect! Turn the page for a preview of *Say You'll Be Mine*, the first book in my NOLA Heart series.

Available Now.

SAY YOU'LL BE MINE PREVIEW

"Need help with those?"

Shaelyn jerked at the familiar masculine voice and nearly pantsed herself. Picking a wedgie in public, while sometimes necessary, was embarrassing, but losing her shorts in front of Brady Taylor, strangers, and the all-seeing eyes of her parish church might actually spell the end of her.

Then again, problem solved. Meme Elaine would have to find someone else to inherit their ancestral home, of course, but Shaelyn could work some serious magic from Upstairs.

"Nope, I've got it," she bit out. She didn't look at him. One glance and there was a decent chance of her good sense going MIA.

"You sure?" Black Nike tennis shoes entered her peripheral vision. "Looks like you might need a hand."

His toned calves were dusted with short, black hairs. It was a sign of weakness, she knew, but Shaelyn couldn't stop the upward progression of her gaze. Settled low on his hips were maroon basketball shorts with cracked-gold lettering running up the side. The first and second O's were missing, so that instead of Loyola, it read "L Y LA." She wondered why he wasn't wearing his alma mater, Tulane University, and then reminded herself that she didn't care. Her gaze traveled up to a faded-blue NOPD T-shirt that—

Shaelyn inhaled sharply as she realized just how awful *she* must look. Boob sweat was the least of her worries when her underwear had officially integrated itself between her butt cheeks. She reached up to smooth her short, curly hair, which she'd tamed with a headband straight out of the '90s. Her bedroom was proving to be a treasure trove of forgotten goodies.

"You've got something . . . " Brady reached out a hand toward her butt.

"Hey!" She swatted at his long-tapered fingers. He wasn't wearing his hat today, and she finally had her first glimpse of his blue-on-blue eyes. She'd once compared them to the crystal blue waters of Destin (where their families once vacationed together in Florida every summer), and she was annoyed to find that time had not dampened their appeal. Straightening her spine, she snapped, "Hands off."

Holding both hands up, he dipped his chin. "You might wanna check out your behind then." Those blue eyes crinkled as he grinned, with small laugh lines fanning out from the corners.

Shaelyn twisted at the waist. Three leaves were stuck to her butt, suctioned to the fabric of her shorts as though hanging on for dear life. Sweat, apparently, was the proper glue foliage needed for attachment.

She was never working out again.

"You got it?" Brady asked, humor lacing his husky drawl. "I'm good with my hands, if you need help."

An image of Brady's large hands cupping her butt

snapped her into action. She swiped at the offending leaves, sending them fluttering to the ground. "I'm good. Thanks."

His sweeping glance, one that traveled from her tennis shoes all the way up to her face, left her wondering if he liked what he saw or if he was glad he'd dumped her years ago. Finally, he murmured, "I can see that."

The key ring came loose from her belt loop with an extra hard tug of desperation, and she started for her car. "Right. Well, nice to see you."

Brady effectively ruined her escape by leaning against her car door with his arms crossed over his hard chest. Hadn't she suffered enough today without having to deal with him, too? Boob sweat, wedgies, and leaves suctioned to her ass were all a woman could take, thank you very much.

She gestured at him. "Do you mind?"

His answering smile was slow and easy. "Not at all."

Her fingers curled tightly around the car keys. "I've got somewhere to be."

"Yeah?" His tone suggested that he didn't believe her. "Where are you going?"

She toyed with the idea of blowing off his question, but if there was one thing she knew about Brady Taylor, it was that he was annoyingly persistent. "I've got a bachelorette party tonight."

"Oh, yeah?" He said it differently this time, as if intrigued, perhaps even despite himself. "Didn't realize you had many friends left in N'Orleans?"

She scowled, placed a hand on her hip, and then realized that she must look about five seconds away from throwing a good ol' Southern princess tantrum. Hastily she folded her arms over her chest to mimic his stance. With determination she ignored the way her sweat-coated skin fused together.

"For the record, I do have friends." She didn't, not really, but he didn't know that. "And secondly, my job is hosting a bachelorette party."

He seemed to digest that, his full mouth momentarily flattening before quirking up in a nonchalant smile. "Where do you work nowadays, Shae?"

The bells of Holy Name chimed again. She really had to be going, but something stopped her from walking around the hood of her car, climbing in, and speeding away. She didn't want to think about what that *something* might be.

"I work at La Parisienne in the French Quarter. On Chartres."

One of his black brows arched up in surprise. "The lingerie joint?"

Only a man would call a business that sold women's underwear a "joint." Rolling her eyes, Shaelyn let her weight rest on her right leg. She bit back another moan of pain. "It has a name, but yes, I work at the 'lingerie joint.'"

"And they host bachelorette parties?"

She shrugged. "Sometimes. Tonight we're cohosting it with The Dirty Crescent."

"The sex toy shop?"

"Yes."

His blue eyes glittered, and when he asked, "Can I come?" his voice slid through her like that first shot of whiskey she'd downed in his grandfather's office years earlier. Shocking at first, and then hot and tingly as it heated her core.

Then he ruined everything by laughing.

Nothing ever changed with him.

"You're such a jerk," she snapped. She stepped forward and pushed at his chest to urge him away from her car. He didn't budge, which only infuriated her. How dare he tease her like he hadn't broken her heart? So what if she'd been young, naïve, and fifty shades of stupid? Being a gentleman was not overrated.

He was still laughing when he caught her by the shoulders. "I could arrest you for harassment." His hands were warm on her exposed skin, hotter, maybe, than the late afternoon sun toasting the back of her neck.

Shaelyn glared up at him, not the least bit pacified by the mischievous glint in his blue eyes. His thumbs stroked her collarbone. Once, twice. If she'd been a weaker woman, she would have curled into his embrace. "You should arrest yourself."

"For what?"

"For being an ass."

His head dipped, his breath a whisper against her ear. Goosebumps teased her flesh. "You gonna do it yourself? Maybe buy a pair of new 'cuffs from that party tonight and put them to good use on me?"

It took a second for the words to sink in, and another second after that to realize that he was taunting her, baiting her for the sort of reaction she would have given him when they were young.

She refused to sink to his level.

Stepping away from his touch, she unlocked her car with her keyless remote. "Have a nice life, Brady."

She congratulated herself on sounding Cool, Calm and Collected, even though her insides were crashing around and threatening to pull a Birds of Paradise Incident Part II. She rounded the front of her car.

"Hey, Shae?"

She glanced up. Standing with his hands on his hips, Brady's eyes were narrowed, his brows drawn together. With that hard expression on his face, it was difficult to think of him as anything but as a cop on a mission. Difficult to remember him as the boy who'd once held her heart.

"Yes, Brady?"

His gaze flicked from her to the busy street. "Tell the fiancé hello for me," he said. And then, just like he had at his grandparent's BBQ, he stalked off without giving her the chance to have the last word.

Jerk.

Want to keep reading? *Say You'll Be Mine* is now available online in both e-book and paperback!

ALSO BY MARIA LUIS

ABOUT THE AUTHOR

Maria Luis is the author of the sexy NOLA Heart and Blades Hockey series.

Historian by day and romance novelist by night, Maria lives in New Orleans, and loves bringing the city's cultural flair into her books. When Maria isn't frantically typing with coffee in hand, she can be found binging on reality TV, going on adventures with her other half and two pups, or plotting her next flirty romance.

⚜

30725032R00151

Printed in Great Britain
by Amazon